T0104880

A Cardiac Arrest

a novel

Donald Motier

authorHOUSE®

AuthorHouse™
1663 Liberty Drive
Bloomington, IN 47403
www.authorhouse.com
Phone: 1 (800) 839-8640

Published by AuthorHouse 09/02/2015

ISBN: 978-1-5049-2800-7 (sc)
ISBN: 9781-5049-2743-7 (e)

Print information available on the last page.

Gentlemen of the jury, the facts are fact but the conclusions are wrong.

- Abraham Lincoln

Above All

- for D.A. & A.M.

Crucified, thrown behind
    barbed wire and stone,
I lived to die for you;
    rejected and alone,
Like a rose trampled
    on the ground,
I took the fall for Love
    and thought about you,
    Above **ALL**.

- Adapted from an anonymous hymn.

Also by Donald Motier

FICTION

Just Friends, A Novella and Two Short Stories

Just Friends, A Love Story

Return To Sónville

The Book of Joel

Unfinished Business

FACTION

Mystic Chords of Memory: The Lost Journal of William Wallace Lincoln (two editions)

Saving Lincoln: Mystic Chords of Memory Part 2

BIOGRAPHY/LITERARY CRITICISM

Gerard: The Influence of Jack Kerouac's Brother On His Life and Writing (two editions)

TRAVEL

On The Trak (two editions)

POETRY

Faces of Being

On the Hound and Other Prose Poems 1970 - 78

Mnemonicons

Co-Incidings: Collected Poems 1965-1999

EDITED BY DONALD MOTIER

The Gray Day and Other Poems by Charles Patton and New Poems 2000-2008 by Donald Motier

The Collected Poems of Charles Penrose Patton 1962-1991

1.

June 11, 2008, 8:17 a.m.

Liberty regained!

David Platon walked out of Shanksville State Prison. The oppressive clang of the cell doors a memory to be burned into his collective consciousness forever.

He felt such momentous relief as he walked to his friend's car--a relief like a ton of insidious weight suddenly, miraculously lifted off his shoulders.

He was keenly aware of the clear, blue sky of this new day, vibrant fields, leaf-filled trees on the hill in the distance. He breathed in the liberty air that seemed so much sweeter and fresher than the steel and concrete incarcerated air he had inhaled for the last ten years-- illusory perhaps but very *real* to David.

Before placing the box containing the few books and toiletries he had brought with him, he hugged the nearest tree for there were no trees in the drab prison interior and walking on the grass plots between the concrete walkways was forbidden.

"You can't imagine what relief I feel -- the weight of all those years melting away," David said to Walt as he got in the front passenger seat of Walt's 2004 Toyota Camry.

"You're right, I can't imagine what you're feeling," Walt replied.

Not far from the prison they stopped at the Santa Losa Restaurant for breakfast. After a delicious (as compared to institutional mass produced food) meal of eggs over lightly, hash browns, Canadian bacon, toast with blueberry jam, tomato juice and coffee, it felt strange for David to be handling money when he paid the bill. Walt had brought along David's wallet from home and of course he had been given his prison account savings and $40 "release money."

"Felt strange handling money," David commented.

"I guess so. Where do you want to go first?" Walt asked.

"To my house first. Haven't been in it in ten years."

As he sat back and relaxed taking in the scenery on the way to his house in Santa Losa, David mused over the political changes that had occurred in the last ten years.

The presidents Bushwhackers had left the newly elected African-American president Barak Obama with the legacy billions in debt for two wars where the nation had been in the black and no wars when Bill Clinton had left office.

It's hypocritical for the Republicans to accuse Democrats of creating the crisis in Iraq. Republicans need to turn the clock back to when Dubya fabricated weapons of evidence of mass destruction and association between the secular Saddam Hussein and the religious fanatic Osama Bin Laden. Saddam (as much a horrorist he was using chemical weapons against the Kurds) was the only person who could defend Iraq against neighboring Iran. Seven years later and the deaths of thousands of US soldiers, Iraqi soldiers, terrorists and civilians, the Iranians and jihadists are about to carve up Iraq. Rather than giving the Bushwhackers, presidential pensions and libraries, we should send them, Dubya, Cheney, Rumsfeld and Wolfowitz to the World Court to be tried as mass murderer war criminals.

David's brick duplex was old-- built around the end of World War I. David's grandfather had bought it in 1921 from the first owner for $1,500, a large sum at that time. It was one of the first dwellings built on a large plot of wooded land owned by Jose Hidalgo, whose family had been one of the first settlers in the area when it was still a part of Mexico. The land had been sold to the city of Santa Losa to extend its northern border as the city grew in the 19th century.

David's father had moved in with his new wife after they were married in June 1935. David's grandmother had died young at age 47 of a stroke at the dinner table on Columbus Day October 10, 1934.

David had inherited the house in 1991 after the death of his father from Alzheimer's in September 1990 at the understaffed, gloom-warehouse called the San Angelo Veteran's Hospital and his mother had died in March 1991 of emphysema after extended ten-month intensive care hospital stay at North Santa Losa Hospital. David received the horrendous bill of $500,000 which half-of had to be written off as his mother's Medicare only covered that part.

Since David was an only child, both deaths following one another in ten months were especially traumatic. He had also lost his beloved 16 1/2 year old pet cat Boo on Good Friday April 1990 and a friend to suicide in May 1990.

David's father was buried in East Santa Losa Cemetery. Like David, his father had been an only child. David's mother had stipulated she did not want to be buried in Santa Losa-- no reason given but there were only three plots in East Santa Losa Cemetery where David's grandparents were buried. David's mother wanted to be buried across the Lost River in the suburban Rolling Hills Cemetery with her mother, stepfather, half-brother already lying under that sod. One plot remained and David had granted her wish. Rolling Hills was one of the newer cemeteries with flat bronze markers and flower holders that could be lifted up. The markers were evenly spaced dividing plots. A few mausoleums of white marble jutted out of the manicured green landscape.

In contrast, East Santa Losa Cemetery dated back to the mid-nineteenth century with the oldest worn sandstone tombstones, monoliths of various sizes and modern stones of marble and granite filling the hillside.

At the funerals, David's extended family consisted of his mother's cousins, stepsisters and stepbrothers and their offspring and a few relatives of his father he'd never met.

His mother's parents had divorced in 1917 when she was seven and her mother had married a widower with six children, His mother, who said she drank a quart of beer every night so she could sleep, had confessed to David one night when he was in his 40s that she had been *interfered with* by her stepbrothers and Daniel was to never tell anyone. He didn't-- till after she died.

One step-cousin at the funeral commented on *how well David was holding up.* David had-- while there was so much to do-- funeral arrangements, burial arrangements, calling relatives, obtaining copies of death certificates, finding and registering wills at the courthouse. He had at least avoided probate by getting his father to sign a power of attorney form and also "selling" the house to David for $1. His mother was already in the hospital at the time.

However, when all was said and done and buried, there was this huge vacuum and the *real* sense of loss set in-- a sense of final abandonment-- three-less loved beings in his life-- self pity and depression-- a deep sense of lonelyhood encompassed him like the dark ominous cloud of an approaching storm.

In addition to the deep wounds of the loss of three of the sentient family member beings, his young son had chose to distribute the latest young person's drug Ecstasy, a newly illegal amphetamine-based drug and got arrested. David partially blamed himself (although his son said it was *his* choice to do it) for failed mentoring and closed doors during the boy's teenaged years- David stuck behind steel, concrete and barbed wire.

Rather than go to a professional to deal with his depression and loss-- not trusting psychobabblists, friends or extended pseudo-family members, he self-medicated by isolating himself in his house and resurrecting and old childhood hobby-- stamp collecting.

David had been divorced years ago in 1981 when his son Joel was five after catching his wife Carol cheating. He occasionally had dinner with a friend but had no desire to date.

The next few years he got into a comfort zone of denial about his tearless, unresolved, unexpressed, repressed mourning and resultant depression and lonelyhood always lurking beneath the surface of his consciousness. Sometimes out of the blue a certain face, smell or voice would mnemonically bring back a flood of memories.

Until the summer of 1997 and the Blonde.

David had a family membership to a community swimming pool, the North Santa Losa Swim Club that he and his son had frequented for years. David enjoyed swimming laps and working on his tan on his days off. David worked as a reference librarian at the North Santa Losa Public Library.

One late August day at the pool he noticed the Blonde for the first time. Blonde had a perfect youthful body. David himself was slim and trim from years of working-out, bicycling and swimming with Joel and at 48 looked years younger.

He couldn't keep his eyes off Blonde.

As he was leaving the pool that day Blonde suddenly looked David's way and smiled-- David returning it-- a surprised blush breaking through his tanned face at the unexpected connection.

2.

Lonelyhood.

Male menopause seeking rejuvenation of youth with vivacious young Blonde equals rationality out the window and accompanied poor impulse control.

Hot 1986 Monte Carlo SS with T-top, sexy maroon with gold racing stripe emblazoned SS on side panels.

Just For Men dyed dark-brown hair and expensive matching hairpiece.

All hoping to appear 30 instead of 48.

This was David's physical, mental and emotional persona on Saturday, August 17, 1997 when Blonde came into his life or more correctly, when he threw caution to the wind and *let* Blonde into his life.

He hoped no one noticed (except Blonde) as he stared transfixed at Blonde's perfect youthful beauty, brown tanned flesh appearing in and out of the water as Blonde hit the volleyball with vigorous agility.

Water droplets glistening off Blonde's body, Blonde exited the pool and to David's astonishment came to a lone towell close to David.

"Hi!" David managed to blurt out when the mystery Blonde he would soon come to know sat up, shaking Blonde locks from side to side and turned to face David, Blonde's huge blue eyes contrasting the bronzed face smiled at David.

"Hi!" Blonde replied showing perfect white teeth.

"Haven't seen you at the pool before-- I'm Dave."

"My mom and I just moved here from Sacramento-- my name's Jamie."

"Welcome to Santa Losa! I watched you play volleyball-- you're very good! Do you play other sports?" David asked, to show interest and hopefully extend the conversation.

"Yes, I was on the swim, soccer and softball teams in Sacramento."

"Why did you move to Santa Losa?"

"My parents got divorced and my dad disappeared-- was not making any support payments. Mom wasn't making enough at WalMart so a friend of her's said she could get her a job here in Santa Losa as a computer technician at INSINC Industries. Mom has a degree in Computer Technology from Sacramento Community College but stayed home working at WalMart part-time so she'd be home when I got home from school. Anyhow, we didn't need the money with dad's salary. So here we are. Mom's friend Janice got us a membership in the pool," Jamie explained.

"Sorry about what you've been through-- especially your dad bailing after the divorce," David said sympathetically.

"Actually my dad disappearing after the divorce, didn't bother me-- he used to beat the crap out of me for nothing-- it was not paying mom for support."

"I hope things will be better here in Santa Losa. If you'd like a *friend, I'm* here for you," David said with perhaps more eagerness than he meant to show.

With a surprised look on his face Jamie thought *can I really trust an adult man after my dad's example* however Jamie desperately wanted and needed a positive adult role model, replied, "I'd like a *friend*, but I'll have to ask mom and you'll have to meet her."

"Where do you live, Jamie?"

"Two blocks away down 34th Street at the corner of Palm Street, 2nd Floor apartment."

"I live close to you at 33rd and Escondito. Is your mom home now?" David asked hopefully.

"Yes, she's off work weekends-- you can walk home with me but I'd like to swim some more first-- come in too!" Jamie, obviously very athletic, glided through the water with very little splashing—David, although he considered himself a good swimmer, could barely keep up as they did laps across the 50 meter pool. Then they engaged in a furious water volleyball game with other young people and adults, Jamie and David's team trashing the other team 21-6. After the game they returned to their towells laying down to dry in the late afternoon sun.

"My mom wants me home by 5, so we'd better leave now," Jamie said, noticing the pool clock on the clubhouse wall read 10 of.

Little was said as they walked the few blocks to Jamie's apartment-- both nervous, and excited anticipating the introductions and first impressions.

Both wondering, however, what Jamie's mother is going to think about, Jamie bringing home this *much older* new friend.

The door opened and a very attractive woman with blonde hair and blue eyes, slim and trim, looking very much like and older version of her offspring.

"Mom, this is David; his towell happened to be next to mine at the pool and we got talking and I told him about dad disappearing after the divorce and us having to move here from Sacramento and stuff. He's a real nice guy and my friend..."

Jamie's mom looked at David quizzically and asked, "Tell me *about yourself* David-- after all this does seem most *unusual*?"

"I'm 48, divorced with a grown son and am on the staff of the Santa Losa Public Library, have a cat and live a few blocks from here at 33rd and Escondito-- I could use some help around my house-- cutting grass, weeding, cleaning-- if he finishes his chores here at home first," David replied, smiling.

"You understand, David, I will need references before I let Jamie hang out with you."

"Of course," David said, and asked for a piece of paper to give her the number of the head librarian and supervisor at the library.

They exchanged phone numbers and she promised to give him a call.

"Are you coming swimming tomorrow, David?"

"Sure-- see you there Jamie. Very nice meeting you," he said to Jamie's mother.

"Likewise, David," she replied.

Walking back to his house David thought, *what* am I doing?- But then thought, Jamie is *so attractive* and I'm lonely as hell-- the warmth of another human being, especially a *young* person, seemed to assuage the lonelyhood of his male menopausal fantasy regaining his lost youth he'd had with the forbidden special friendship he'd had in 1966 with another Blonde.

When David arrived at the pool a little after 1 p.m. the next day Sunday, Jamie was already there sitting on his towell at the same place waving and smiling.

"Hi David! Mom called the library an everything's cool!"

"That's great, Jamie!" David said not trying to hide his exuberant enthusiasm and relief at the news. "You can call me Dave, Jamie, everybody does."

They swam and played water volleyball for two hours and rested on their towels. David noticed the droplets of water drying on the bronze-tanned perfect young body and felt a guilty/pleasant stirring that he tried unsuccessfully to repress-- hoping that, if Jamie woke up he wouldn't notice. Perhaps sensing David's stirring, Jamie suddenly sat up, smiled and shortly had a noticeable stirring of his own. For a few minutes nothing was said then Jamie put his hand on David's wrist and said, "Let's go to your place-- I'd like to see it and your cat- we had one once but my dad was mean to it and it ran away," with a pleading in his voice and blushing showing through his bronzed countenance, blue eyes gleaming.

Entering David's house, his gray tabby cat Toughie greeted them both, immediately accepting this new person in David's life as if saying, "He's with my David, so he must be OK." Jamie kneeled down and petted Toughie who began to instantly purr approvingly.

"Looks like you've made a friend-- Toughie doesn't usually warm up to new people in her domain that quickly."

"She's beautiful-- I miss my cat Ginger a lot." Then looking around the living room Jamie noticed David's five bookshelves and commented, "You sure have a lot of books."

"I guess it comes with being a librarian and a writer. Do you like to read, Jamie?"

"Oh, yes-- science fiction and history, mostly."

"Well, that's interesting-- those are my favorites, too!" Jamie peeked in the dining room and kitchen and asked, "Can I see the upstairs now?"

"Sure, Jamie,"

Jamie looked around for a minute and sat down on David's bed grinning.

David sat next him.

David lay back on the bed unable to control the stirring bulge in his swim trunks.

Then he felt Jamie's hand rubbing.

When it was over and he was holding the beautiful young naked boy in his arms, David, said, "You know we shouldn't have done that-- I'm very sorry Jamie."

"Nothing to be sorry about-- I *wanted* to do it-- I've known I was Gay as long as I can remember-- I had a lover a few years older back in Sacramento and I fell in love with you at first sight."

"But it's illegal and I'm old enough to be your father,"

"Who cares about age? You're very handsome."

"Jamie we will have to be very careful-- they'll *crucify* me and force you into counseling if we're found out!"

"Nothing will happen! Nobody will know!" Jamie said boldly and confidently blinded by youthful love and innocence.

"Does your mom know you're Gay?"

"No-- she's clueless-- wouldn't be ready to accept yet. I think my dad knew-- or suspected and that's why he beat me up-- often calling me a little faggot!" Jamie said angrily.

"Well, *no one* is going to hurt you now! I love you too!" David said, surprising himself with the commitment and vehemence in his voice.

3.

Jamie came to David's house Wednesdays after school and they made love. He also came Saturday mornings. He cut the grass and later in the fall raked leaves. He would also do routine cleaning-- running the sweeper and dusting.

After that they made love.

On Saturdays they would have lunch at either McDonalds or Burger King. Jamie especially loved the chicken tenders at Burger King that he would drench in ketchup often leaving the bottle at the table half-empty. Nowadays both fast food restaurants only give out the small packs of condiments-- guess it got too expensive as people were using up the bottles or stealing them.

Afternoons, if the weather cooperated, they passed football, biked the 15 mile Santa Losa Bike Trail that encircled the city or hiked in the foothills of the Sierra Nevada Mountains, always on the lookout for mountain lions. Only last year one had came to a campground and dragged a six-yr-old cub scout away.

David's coworkers at the library noticed how happy he seemed and said he must have found a nice woman to date. David only smiled and said nothing.

The months passed and the Christmas holidays arrived.

David bought Jamie a pair of expensive roller blades that were all the rage that year. David bought a cheap pair for himself but was unable to master roller blading anymore than he could roller skating as a boy. However, he could ice skate very well, that is figure skate, even skating backwards and took Jamie along to the new Northside Rink that had opened the previous year. Jamie had never ice skated before but soon mastered it.

David was a little embarrassed when Jamie insisted they skate holding hands around the rink to the rock musing blaring from the loudspeakers feeling they were being stared at as the boy was *pretty old* to be holding hands with his *dad*.

Jamie was oblivious commenting it was cool and *romantic*.

David spent New Year's Eve with Jamie and his mom-- Jamie toasting in the New Year at midnight saying confidently, "*This year* is going to be the *best* of my life."

David had an odd forboding this would not be true.

4.

It was about 10 a.m. Monday morning January 3, 1998 when the two men approached David on duty at the reference desk of Santa Losa Public Library.

"Are you David Platon?" One of the two suited-men asked ignoring the sign in front of the desk stating David Platon.

"Yes, how may I help you?"

"I'm Detective Garnish and this is Detective Ghoul," the bespectled rotund older one said pointing to the short Napoleonic one with cold eyes. "We're from the Santa Losa Police Department and would like to ask you about your relationship with a young boy named Jamie Peyret?"

"What about him?" David said rather defensively, his reddening face betraying his shock and anxiety.

"Not here, Mr. Platon-- we'd like you to come down to the station with us-- don't worry-- just routine questioning," Garnish said in a fake apologetic tone.

Ghoul didn't say anything-- just stared at David accusingly with cruel black eyes as if David was a serial killer.

David told the Head Librarian that something came up regarding his house and he wouldn't be back the rest of the day.

Miss Abraham, the longstanding Head Librarian said, "No problem, David-- I hope everything is all right at your house."

"I'm sure it will be," David replied glancing rather defiantly at the two detectives.

Once at the station the detectives escorted David into the typical-looking windowless interrogation room always shown on the TV cop shows. A lone table with three chairs, one for David on one side and the other two for the detectives. A lone bright light bulb hung from the ceiling over the center of the table. An ash tray and pitcher of water with paper cups were the only other items on the table.

"How long have you known Jamie Peyret?" Garnish inquired.

"Since last August-- we met at the North Santa Losa Swim Club pool-- but I'm sure you already know that. I don't understand why you're interested-- I'm like a big brother to Jamie?" David said vehemently. Regaining his composure after the initial shock of confrontation at the library,

"We received a complaint that there may be inappropriate contact between you and the young boy," Garnish said more as a question-- both cops staring at David to see any guilty reaction.

"Well-- I don't know who would *think* such a thing, but it's an absolute lie-- who was it anyway?" David said looking them both in the eye.

"We're not at liberty to tell you-- because of possible retaliation," Ghoul said.

"No use lying! He told us everything," Ghoul said obviously enjoying himself.

David pretended to look shocked, realizing they were playing the *good cop-bad cop* routine lying-- used to gain confessions from naive suspects.

"That's a lie! Unless you threatened and intimidated Chris-verbally and emotionally abusing him to get a false confession," David retorted.

Ghoul stood up threateningly and yelled, "In the old days I'd have you up against the wall!"

"Charge me with something or let me go!" David said.

"You can go, but don't leave town-- we'll be continuing the investigation-- we *know* something *illegal* is going on and we'll *prove* it," Garnish said.

As David got up to leave, Ghoul said sarcastically, "Have a nice day."

The next day, Tuesday, David went to the office of an attorney, Jim Donkle, he'd heard about who charged reasonable fees to represent controversial clients.

He called the court and told David that, as of yet, no charges had been filed and to lay low and that he would call David if anything came of the investigation.

He didn't ask David if anything illegal had happened between David and Jamie.

David tried to call Jamie the next day, Wednesday, at 4:30 p.m. when the boy didn't show up at 4:00 as usual for their rendezvous, but a woman not Jamie's mother answered, anxiety obvious in the slightly shaking tone of her voice.

David hung up immediately.

He was very worried about Jamie-- especially what he might *do* to himself if he thought David betrayed him.

Desperate, he hid in the bushes outside Jamie's school on the next day, Thursday, to try to intercept him and warn Jamie of the devious ways the Neo-Nazi Sexual Police would try to lie and trick the boy into confessing.

Jamie never showed up, obviously not attending school that day.

David didn't sleep at all that night and dragged himself to the library after downing three cups of strong black coffee.

At 9:00 a.m. his library office phone rang. It was Attorney Donkle who said, "David, you'd better come to my office right away."

5.

"David, they've brought charges against you. I need to know if they're *true*?" Attorney Donkle asked.

"Well--*yes*--but it was a loving, consensual relationship-- he's Gay and I'm Bi and we both *knew* it was illegal but we were *deeply in love*. I know how it looks but age was not a factor," David explained-- hoping for understanding.

"None of that matters to them-- they look it strictly by the *letter* of the law," Donkle said firmly.

"The bastards must have lied to Jamie saying I confessed!"

"They did say he confessed," Donkle said.

"What exactly am I being charged with?"

"Two felonies and a misdemeanor:

Count 1. Statutory Rape

Count 2. Involuntary Deviate Sexual Intercourse

Count 3. Corrupting The Morals Of A Minor."

"What the hell is *involuntary deviate sexual intercourse*?" David asked, incredulous.

"That's legalese for oral or anal sex with a person under the age of 18," Donkle said.

"What's *deviate* about it?-- straight and Gay couples do it all the time-- so it's *not* deviate anymore at the magic age of 18?," David asked in disbelief.

"I agree-- but *it is what it is*-- the most serious charge is the IDSI with a sentence of 5-10 yrs., Statutory Rape carries a 21/2 - 5 and CMM 1 -2-- I'll try to get them all run concurrent by negotiating a plea of no contest-- you don't want Jamie forced to testify."

"I definitely wouldn't want him to go through that! I'm worried he might try to *hurt himself-- if you know what I mean--* I hope they will watch him closely and get him counseling," David said, near tears.

"They wanted to arrest you at the library today but I got them to do it at the preliminary hearing today at Magistrate Sauer's Office at 2 p.m."

At the preliminary hearing Daniel pleaded not guilty, a standard practice at that time, and was granted bail $25,000 secured with the stipulation he has no contact with minors.

The next day Saturday, January 8, 1998 the *Santa Losa Sentinel* had a short one paragraph story in the State & Local Section titled "Santa Losa man, 48, arrested on morals charges..."

6.

Shame.

Embarrassment, paranoia.

David exited and entered his house by the back door and parked his car on the side street Escondito.

Before he could be fired he retired from the Santa Losa Public Library.

He rarely left his house except to go to the grocery store several miles outside of town where he was not known.

The prosecution and Donkle both sought continuances and the case dragged on for months till June. When Donkle convinced David to accept a guilty plea deal he'd arranged with the D.A. that ran all three counts concurrent. On June 11 he was sentenced by Judge Henry Clarkson to 5-10 yrs. in a state correctional institution.

Since Shanksville State Correctional Institution was full David sat at the Santa Losa County Jail for a month till finally transferred to Shanksville.

David learned later that defendants are advised to plead no contest or guilty, *not* for a lesser sentence as the defense attorneys state, but to save the court money paying jurors and taking up court time. Plea deals were arranged over martinis with the defense attorney, district attorney and judge over lunch. For example: The district attorney will tell the defense attorney (with the judge's approval) to tell the defendant that if he goes to trial he'll get 10-20 (a *lie*) so he'd better take the plea bargain offer of 5-10.

With the growing "War on Sex Offenders" that started in the 1970a with the day care scandals, most of which were later found to be hysteria-inflamed false rumors, then the priest scandals of the 1980s where altar boys and others came out of the woodwork claiming (most falsely) they were abused years ago and sued the Catholic church cashing in on the hysteria. Then murder of six-yr-old Megan Kanka in New Jersey led to the knee-jerk sex panic rush to pass new laws against the perceived threat-epidemic of rapists, pedophiles and child molesters lurking around every corner when the actual fact is that most child abusers are family members or close family friends-- not the "stranger danger" scary man in a trenchcoat hanging around parks and playgrounds which amount to only *1% of cases.*

Shanksville State Prison was fifty miles northeast of Santa Losa in the Sierra Nevada Mountains. There had been a riot at Shanksville in October 1990 that started in the dining hall by the inmates allegedly angered by the poor quality and small portions of food served. It soon spread throughout the prison with inmates starting fires on the blocks and other building. The National Guard had to be called in to assist the State Police in quelling the riot which made national news.

The ruins were torn down and in 1991 new modular units were erected separated by fences each with its own yard in addition to the large main yard that was untouched by the destruction. Sex offenders were housed separately in a Mod where they could be treated without fear of violence or harassment by other inmates. Other than child murderers sex offenders (all lumped together by the majority of stereotyping hate-filled inmates as "baby rapers") were at the bottom of the prison hierarchy.

David felt safe in the S.O. Unit and soon fell into the prison routine. He was assigned to work in the library because of his college degree and experience in that field. He also had to endure several "therapeutic" groups to complete his required DOC prescriptive program in order to have a chance of making parole on his minimum in five years.

These groups included *Breaking Barriers, Victim Awareness, Violence Prevention* (sex offenses, even consensual ones as in David's case were labeled "sexually violent" by the conservative, profiling, stereotyping prison psycho-establishment- and Republicans who pushed through such legislation feeding public sex panic to get elected or stay in office) and of course the *Sex Offender Program* itself that was based on a cognitive behaviorist concept that if you change an offender's thinking you can change behavior. This may work in some cases but for true MAPS (minor attracted persons) prison only makes them worse and just like Gay, straight or bisexual orientation cannot be changed. Only community-based treatment programs that help MAPS channel their age-illegal attractions in socially accepted avenues will work. Note that in Europe the age of consent is 12 in The Netherlands if not exploitive, 13 in Spain, 14 in Hungary, Austria, Estonia and Kosovo where the American idea that minors cannot psychologically consent till they reach the *magic* age of 18 to sexual relations with adults is disputed.

The prison SOP was a three-stage program spread over eighteen months that included mandatory attendance, mandatory admittance of one's crime, a detailed, honest sexual history presented before the group with feedback and relapse prevention skills.

All the prison "treatment" programs are funded by the state for the Dept. of Corrections as a cosmetic appeasement of the politicians and uniformed public and did not (as David soon found out) result in parole for most sex offenders. Although David's attorney had optimistically predicted that if David "kept his nose clean" and "do your programs" he could be out on pre-release in 2-3 years. However, after Megan Kanka's murder by a sex offender in 1995 pre-release and parole had dropped from 65% to 35% and a federal incentive was passed that if states' departments of corrections and parole boards kept violent offenders and most sex offenders (violent or not) incarcerated for 80% of their sentences the states would get additional federal funding. David actually found a copy of this bill in the prison law library.

When David came up for parole in 2003 he was given a "hit" (one year denial of parole) till 2004 with the "green sheet" (paperwork from Parole Board stating result of Board's decision and reason for denial) stating only "continue sex offender program." The same result happened in 2005. Then in 2006 with only two years left to "max" (complete his 5-10 yrs. sentence) he was awarded "post-pre-release" by the DOC because they felt the Parole Board was unfair in continually denying parole to David when he had actually completed all required programs and had no misconducts, thus over-ruling the Parole Board. It was called post-pre-release because it is normally granted before or around one's minimum sentence expiration.

David's long-time friend Walt, to whom he'd given power-of-attorney to look after his affairs while incarcerated, picked him up at the prison on October 5, 2006 and delivered him to the Santa Losa Community Corrections Center on Esperanza Street in a seedy section of downtown. Also known as a "halfway house," David was to stay there till paroled. He was required to find a job, pay nominal rent, purchase his own food to be cooked and consumed at the facility kitchen, go to a S.O. group twice a week and was permitted out of the center to go to group, church on Sundays, grocery shopping and the Goodwill of Salvation Army stores for clothing. Visitors were permitted 9 a.m. to 5 p.m. and 6 p.m. to 9 p.m. seven days a week.

David found a part-job at the New Directions Bookstore on Bonanza Street, a five-minute walk from the center.

He attended the twice-a-week hour and a half S.O. group at Compressor Psychological Associates on the on the other side of the city ironically only eight blocks from his house in North Santa Losa and a block from the North Branch Santa Losa Public Library. It was a forty-five minute walk from the center and good exercise and he could always take the 25th Street bus in bad weather or hitch a ride from one of the guys at the center who had a car.

As part of the process for making parole for sex offenders, David had to pass a polygraph (not admissable in court under normal circumstances) costing an exorbitant fee of $300, ridiculous for offenders struggling to get on their feet financially. According to the Parole Board, this polygraph was especially *modified* to test for sex offender compliance such as sexual or other unauthorized contact with minors. David passed with flying colors and the person who was administering the polygraph stated, "You sure hate lying." David was recommended for parole by the Center and Compressor Associates.

David was ecstatic telling himself *I'm finally going home*!

The parole interview in October 2007 had seemed to go well-not the hostile intonations of the interrogators he had experienced during the incarceration interviews.

On October 23, about two weeks after the parole interview, when he'd just got back from work at the bookstore at 5:15 p.m., he was called into the center manager's office. Mr. Intaglio, a bespectacled men in his

’50s with a deeply-lined face, said, looking apologetic, “I’m sorry, David but the Parole Board has denied you parole and the C.C.C. policy dictates I must send you back to Shanksville on A.C. (administrative custody) status.”

7.

Immediately a counselor came into the office with 'cuffs and he was escorted to a waiting van and before he knew what was happening he was back in a cell at Shanksville-- this time in the "hole" RHU (Restrictive Housing Unit) unjustly. Not only those inmates who received misconducts and deserved to be there in solitary confinement 24/7 other than a short shower three times a week and an hour a day recreation period in small outdoor cages that was never given, other inmates like David were stuck there in the limbo of A.C. status.

David had to wear an orange jumpsuit and was given only toilet paper, miniature toothbrush and small tube of toothpaste, a towell, one sheet and ratty blanket. The toilet leaked and ants infested the cell. A light in the ceiling remained on 24/7 and the inmates were fed through a small opening in door of the cellcages. David imagined what zoo animals must have experienced in the old zoos where they had no yard and were continually on display in small cages.

He languished there for two weeks (it was supposed to be one but he was somehow forgotten-- just another number) till his old Unit Manager, Ms. Zarnow, also head of the S.O. Program Block he had lived in for eight years arranged to get him returned to her block. She was livid-- furious at the Parole Board, who, even though David did everything required to be paroled AGAIN, even passing the $300 fifteen minute polygraph, denied him again with the same BS reason on the green sheet "continue S.O. Group...". David's new attorney, Mr. Belscher, wrote the Board several letters requesting a specific reason for the denial but received only form letters stating the Board did not have to release specific information. It wasn't till years later that David found out the real reason he was denied parole at the halfway house. It seems that at that time, 1997, pre-release status inmates in a halfway house did NOT have to register with the State Police on the Megan's Law web site as they were still considered DOC inmates. Only those people on parole or released at the expiration of their maximum sentence had to register. Therefore, even though David passed the polygraph that PROVED he had no sexual or other contact with minors while at the halfway house, the Board was fearful that the fact there were un-registered (s)ex offenders running around loose and the public found out they, the DOC and politicians would be in deep trouble.

All Ms. Zarnow asked so he could stay on the unit was that he be a group facilitator for a S.O. related program. David chose a four-part course "Empathy and Compassionate Action" that had four workbooks he purchased himself and was started by two Vermont corrections psychologists that on follow-up studies showed a remarkably low recidivism rate.

The idea of emphasizing the long-term effects of in particular rape, incest and forcible child molesting and pedophilia such as drug addiction, alcoholism, inability to trust people, low self-esteem, eating disorders, marital problems and even suicide on victims and *keeping* those effects in the forefront of one's consciousness when released should go a long way in keeping most offenders (other than conscious-lacking sociopaths) from reoffending.

David felt a sense of redemption for being able to help inmates who really chose to change behavior that hurt others and themselves and had not benefitted from the cognitive behaviorism group.

David saw the Parole Board again in January 2008 and with six months to go to max they finally offered parole.

David told them in so many words to *shove it where the sun doesn't shine.*

8.

June 11, 2008, 10:28 a.m.

David entered his house for the first time in ten years.

Time and the dust of years of neglect had taken its toll.

Boxes of books he had sent home sat next to bookshelves in the living room. Some of the yellowed wallpaper (from years of his parents' smoking) had begin to peel and the now gray-colored very worn rug thinly covered the hardwood floor.

In contrast, the small dining room had freshly painted white walls and a brownish-red shag carpet-- on of the few improvements made by Darla, a former tenant.

While at the Santa Losa County Jail in 1998 a neighbor woman, Darla, with three kids whom he had been friendly with had written to him and asked if she and her kids could stay at his house as a house-sitter agreeing to pay the utilities and make improvements in lieu of paying rent till she got on her feet and got a job, Her alcoholic carpenter husband had left her and she was about to be evicted from her rented house. She and her sons, fourteen and sixteen had evidently done the work in the dining room (and upstairs front bedroom walls that had been painted white) but that was all.

David soon learned that he had made a big mistake. Darla had not paid any of the utility bills (throwing them in the wastebasket according to ther one son Arty whom David had talked to on the phone) and falsely claimed she was homeschooling (she also had a 12-yr-old daughter) instead was running around drinking and whoring at night. David also learned she was schizophrenic and not taking her medicine-- a fact he learned from a mutual psychologist friend.

David had to contact Walt, who had power-of-attorney for David's affairs, Dr. Glenn Williams his psychologist friend and the kids' biological father who had tried unsuccessfully to gain custody for years but the court had always granted it to pretty Darla who charmed the judge. Since there was no lease, she was given thirty days to be off the premises or face arrest.

The oldest son moved out and disappeared and later David heard he's joined the Army. This time the biological father got custody of the two remaining kids Arty and his sister Anne and took them to live with him in a town fifty miles south of Santa Losa.

David's house was vacant for the remaining nine years of his incarceration in the zoohell.

The ancient kitchen stove that had been his parents and and dated from the 1950s was unusable so he bought a new one from Harris Electric and Gas.

The basement was a mess. Darla was a hoarder and boxes and boxes-- many wet and falling apart full of junk, papers and old clothes littered the floor-- same with the attic where he even found an arrest warrant for Darla for a DUI.

The old gas furnace that dated from the 1970s and had replaced a coal-burning one, had deteriorated and was unsafe and unusable.

David was fortunate that he was able to have it replaced free of charge and also have the house weatherized by a government grant from a program for low-income homeowners.

Although David had his driver's license renewed, he didn't have the money to buy a car (his old 1988 Trans-Am had been stolen and never recovered) and relied on riding the city bus for transportation.

Walt took him to buy groceries, new sheets, blankets and pillow case. The ancient Frigidaire refrigerator from the 1950s still worked after being plugged in. David thought they don't make appliances like they used to-- Nowadays they all have a built-in obsolescence so after a few years you were forced to buy a new one.

9.

David had been away ten years and missed most of the technological advances. In November 1997 he purchased an early cell phone, a Tandy, bulky and heavy-- expensive at $100 from Radio Shack in the North Santa Losa strip mall.

That had disappeared along with his Pentax 35mm camera, lenses and carrying case. Further inventory of his possessions revealed his stamp collection, 1957 Milwaukee Braves Topps baseball card collection (1957 was the year the Braves had beat the Yankees in the World Series)-- that Braves team had such stars as sluggers Hank Aaron and Eddie Mathews and Hall of Fame pitcher Warren Spahn, a pink opaque piece of Carnival glass vase, 1904 brass Ivy League baseball trophy, Civil War miniballs and some record albums and books-- all probably stolen by schizo Darla when kicked out of David's house.

David's friend Walt said that Darla had married twice more, had a son (whom she lost custody of) to a used car salesman and divorced and married a Hindu man and was somewhere in New Mexico.

Water over the damn-- just *material things*-- got to move on, David reasoned. My fault trusting her but it had been mainly so her kids weren't thrown out on the street homeless.

10.

A few days after he came home and after purchasing a 2008 lightweight Verizon cell phone and notifying remaining family (some had bailed after his arrest) and friends, Dr. Johan Summer, a long-time friend and Professor Emeritus of Philosophy from Berkeley, called and invited him to attend a Writers Conference in San Francisco in on June 14. Dr. Summer lived with his wife Dr. Aice Summer in their new home on Tree Top Lane in rural Carmet Twp. about ten miles from Santa Losa. He was working on a historical novel about Robert E. Lee and the Battle of Gettysburg and Alice was working on a collection of poems.

David was also working on a book he had started while on sabbatical (incarcerated) based on his great-grandfather's Civil War service for the Union stationed first as a guard at the White House (then called the Executive Mansion) in 1861-62 and had met the Lincoln family and was befriended by Willie Lincoln, the president's son. This was, of course, before David's ancestors had moved to California after the Civil War from Pennsylvania.

The guest speaker at the Writers Conference, which is an annual gathering of writers published and unpublished that featured workshops on every genre of writing from literary fiction to romance novel writing, was none other than Jean Carter Wheatley prolific psychological-realist novelist who was a distinguished professor of English at UCLA. She was David's favorite contemporary novelist of that genre. He had originally met Jean when she spoke at graduate a English class at Berkeley in 1973 at the invite of a professor friend of David's. Jean was still beautiful in her 60s, slim with long-dark, almost black hair and those dark-brown doe eyes that seemed to look right through you saying *I know you.* After the conference dinner and a Q and A session with Jean in which David was one of the few to ask an intelligent one-- at the following autograph session David asked if he could have his picture taken with her and she graciously accepted. While she was autographing her latest novel, *The Funeral Director's Daughter*, David mentioned that yesterday had been his birthday. She smiled warmly and as David took the book she closed her hand gently over his. David never forgot that kind gesture.

At the time, David hadn't known that her devoted husband had died only five months previously and she now lived alone near the UCLA campus in a house sorrow-filled with memories and ghosts of the past.

11.

To bring himself up to date and technologically correct for the 21st century 2008, David bought a new pocket-size Kodak digital camera and memory card that held up to 165 images, 27" digital TV with DVD included, Toshiba laptop computer and Hewlett-Packard printer/scanner/copier.

He decided to forgo buying a car as persons fifty-five and over could ride free on the SLTA (Santa Losa Transit Authority) bus routes by showing a card provided by the company. One stop was right across 33rd St. diagonally from his house and took him into center city. Another route ran only a few blocks south on 31st Street and also took him to center city. The north branch of the Santa Losa Public Library and the Sierra Health Center Hospital were only a few more blocks south on 31st. The first time he rode the bus he felt paranoidly that everyone on the bus *knew* that he was a (s)ex offender.

David soon taught himself WordPerfect and PhotoShop and related tools of the computer. He really enjoyed the error-free clean text he printed out and ability to clean-up and doctor images. Gone were the days of White-Out, correction tape and ink erasers.

The remaining autumn of 2008 and winter-spring of 2009 David spent several hours most mornings writing his Civil War "faction" (*a type of literature in which real events are used as the basis for a fictional story*).

Some mornings he visited the north branch of the Santa Losa Public Library for Google research on his book and then on nice days walked the 2½ miles from his house along the scenic Wapinoma River Path to center city.

On weekends he'd have dinner with a friend, usually Walt, and they's take in a movie. In the spring of 2009 David started to attend the games of the Santa Losa AAA minor league baseball team the Indians whose ballpark was on beautiful City Island in the middle of the Wapinoma River. Being with a crowd of people made him temporarily feel less lonely--as if he *belonged* in the community and not a pariah.

12.

While at the halfway-house in 2006-07 David had met an older woman, Dolores Hatchkins, at Wesley Union Church a few blocks away from the half-way house in downtown Santa Losa. She was ten years older than him at 68 but intelligent, spry and friendly, Dolores was originally from Arizona but moved to Santa Losa in 2003 at the suggestion of her sister Florence after the death Dolores's husband the previous year. Ironically, she was a retired paralegal whose late husband had been an ambulance chaser.

After David had attended a few services, Dolores invited him to dinner at her apartment on the 10th floor of the Flora Apartments, a high-rise for the elderly on 2nd Street. David had to decline because of the half-way house restrictions. The first two times Dolores invited him he simply told her he had *other plans.* Being no fool, she asked if he had a wife, girlfriend or was Gay. None of the above David told her and then explained...briefly... his *crime* and halfway-house restrictions.

Expecting her to do a sex-panic bolt and not speak to him again was the paranoia he experienced and was reflective of the nature of his digital scarlet letter Megan's Law registration online.

She didn't.

Another irony was that her daughter had married a paroled sex offender with similar charges to David's-- a consensual relationship with a person under eighteen.

Although he could not visit her at her apartment, she started visiting him at the halfway-house bringing cookies, iced tea and her scrabble board.

Their friendship continued till that fateful day when David had returned from his part-time job at the New Directions Bookstore downtown and was immediately 'cuffed and sent back to Shanksville on AC status.

However, Dolores wrote to him (after David wrote and explained his sudden disappearance from church). Before David "maxed-out" in 2008 Dolores and Walt did some general cleaning at David's house.

After his release, David would often walk or take the bus to center city and have lunch with her at a favorite restaurant.

The only thing David didn't like was the small cramped elevator ride to Dolores's 10th floor apartment-- suffering the residual claustrophobic reaction after years of living in a 4 x 8 cell.

Gradually David began to notice physical and mental changes in Dolores. She put on weight, seemed unsteady on feet, had minor hand tremors and memory problems, and uncharacteristically, pressed David for sex even though he had made it clear he was only interested in friendship.

He urged her to see a physician who diagnosed her with rapidly developing Parkinson's disease.

As Dolores's memory problems worsened (she had got lost at the Raspberry Food Court when she got up to get a refill on her coke and although the soda fountain was only about 20 feet away, wandered around the food court with a perplexed lost look on her face forcing David to rescue her and kept misplacing keys and money). David began to feel more like a caretaker than a friend. With his own issues of trying to readjust to the community, it became too stressful and he had to break off the relationship.

Dolores had a son in Pennsylvania and David called him and explained the situation. Arrangements were made and she moved to Pennsylvania to live with her son.

13.

In the meantime he had made a few other acquaintances while doing research for his book in the north branch of the Santa Losa library.

On day an attractive, petite young woman and two tall young men all appearing to be college age settled down around a computer next to David. He immediately noticed they were speaking a foreign language that sounded like Russian. David smiled when the young woman looked his way with a expression that said "can you help me?"

Surprisingly, in perfect English, she asked the for the address of a particular website. He got up, went over and gave her the address. She thanked him with a beautiful smile.

It turned out her name was Lira, she was twenty-two. She, along with her companions were graduate students on an exchange program from Tatarstan in Russia's central Asian region. Tatarstan, home of the Tatars, was a Russian "republic." In the 13th century their ancestors the Tartars had conquered much of Asia and eastern Europe. They were fierce horsemen fighters similar to the Huns and Mongols. The language he'd heard the group speaking was actually Turkic. Only Lira spoke English fluently. David found her attractive, exotic, intelligent and interesting to talk to. One day she asked if he lived nearby but although David said *yes*, he never followed-up on what could have been an invite for intimacy by the look in her eye.

The other acquaintance was Tom, a tall retired high school English teacher who often sat at the computer next to David in the library. David struck a conversation with Tom over their mutual interests in literature, sports and history. They attended a few Santa Losa Indians baseball games on City Island and a fall guided tour of historic Santa Losa Cemetery. Founded in the early 1800s, it held the remains of the famous and infamous citizens from the city's past of Native Americans, Mexicans, pioneers, gold miners and scoundrels.

It turned out Tom was, like David, a Civil War buff who had ancestors that fought for the Union from Tom's home state of Maryland, although some had also fought for the Confederacy, Maryland was a state with divided loyalties that divided families often with tragic results.

Tom had been planning a trip back to Baltimore to visit his older brother who was not well and invited David to accompany him suggesting that they could visit several Civil War battlefield sites.

David gladly accepted as he had also been planning to visit Georgetown and the Ball's Bluff Battlefield near Leesburg, Virginia in conjunction with David's research for his *factional* book based on his great-grandfather's experiences while bivouacked at the White House (then called the Executive Mansion) in 1861-62 and his friendship with President Lincoln's son William "Willie" Wallace Lincoln.

After stopping in Baltimore to visit Tom's brother who was suffering from bladder cancer that metastisized and was not to live more than six months, they rented a car and drove south to Leesburg, Virginia, a friendly, quaint southern town where nearby on October 21, 1861 Colonel Edward D. Baker a close family friend of the Lincoln's who was devoted to Willie, was killed in the Battle of Ball's Bluff.

David and Tom toured the site that was basically just a small clearing at the top of a heavily-wooded cliff overlooking the Potomac River obscured by thick summer foliage. There were separate small monuments honoring both Union and Confederate fallen and a central one with Colonel Baker's name and dates and U.S. flag, supposedly marking the spot where he fell.

From there they backtracked north, crossed the bridge over the Potomac at Point-of-Rocks, turned right and followed a scenic route paralleling the river in Maryland all the way into Georgetown and Oak Hill Cemetery where Willie Lincoln lay in the tomb of Lincoln friend William Thomas Carroll from February 24, 1862 till April 20, 1865 when Willie's coffin was removed from the tomb and taken (on a wagon for $10) to the train to join his father on the long mournful trip home to Springfield.

Willie had been only eleven (turned eleven December 21, 1861) when he died on Friday, February 20, 1862 about 5 p.m. of typhoid and smallpox. His funeral was the only occasion other than a president's that the government was shut down. A perfect clone of his father-- empathic, sensitive, intellectually and morally precocious-- he was deeply loved by all and sorely missed.

The William Thomas Carroll tomb was located at the far northwest corner of Oak Hill Cemetery in Georgetown, a hilly section of the District of Columbia bordering Washington on the south. Although a path meandered toward the center of the vast city of the dead, Tom and David decided to *tombwhack* northwest over increasingly older and leaning or broken monuments. Ancient oaks and elms (planted in the late 1840s to beautify the grounds-- cemetery opened in 1850) encircled with vines gave the eerie impression of going back in time till they finally reached the tomb. A precipitous drop of about forty feet led down to Rock Creek below. Only about six feet of ground lay in front of the rusted, six-inch thick, square-holed, thick-chained door with a huge old iron lock.

David peered through the door and could read the various names of those interred in the crypts on the wall, mostly those of actual Carroll family members. A narrow, three-foot, green and brown tiled floor lay in front of the crypts David thought this would have not been very much room for the six-foot-four president and Willie's opened coffin to rest when allegedly the president visited a couple of times the week after Willie's death to gaze a few more times on his beloved son's countenance.

Incredibly, David could see drag marks on the floor leading from a bottom empty crypt possibly when Willie's coffin was removed in 1865 to join his father on the funeral train back to Springfield or during the president's visits in 1862.

David had brought along a panasonic mini-tape recorder and after turning it on to record, placed it in one of the square holes in the door. After a few minutes it stopped recording even though David had made sure there were fresh batteries in it.

Before leaving, Tom took David's picture by the tomb with David pointing to a white rose he had placed in one of the square holes in the door. David also took some ivy that had grown ove the top of the tomb.

When David got back home to Santa Losa the next day he played back the tape that suddenly began to play through and was shocked to hear a young boy's voice softly but clearly ask "Dave?"

David checked the cemetery registry of burials in the Carroll tomb but there was no boy ever entombed there Willie's age-- the younger of Carroll's sons had died at age five and another at nineteen-- no boy whose voice could have sounded like a eleven-yr-old like the mystery boy asking quietly for "Dave?"

Research into Willie's known friends in Washington revealed no one named Dave. That EVP (electronic voice phenomena) remains a mystery. If indeed, it was the voice of Willie Lincoln heard, it was for the first time in 146 years. Could it be that the Dave the voice was referring to was he, David Platon?

It was an irrefutable fact witnessed by Tom, that one, new batteries had been put in the tape recorder before the trip, two, a blank tape had been loaded and three, the tape had inexplicably stopped recording at the tomb (as if some invisible energy source was draining energy from it-- a common occurrence reported by paranormal investigators) but played through when David got home.

14.

David had one cousin, Cynthia, who, along with her family, were non-judgmental and had supported David through his ordeal.

Cynthia invited him for Thanksgiving and Christmas dinners in 2008 and these delicious home-cooked meals and accompanied socialization mad him feel like part of a family again.

David wondered as the clock struck 12 on New Year's Eve what the next year would bring.

15.

Through the fall and winter of 2008 and spring of 2009 David worked on the manuscript of his book based on his great-grandfather's Civil War experience as a Union sergeant bivouacked on the White House lawn as a guard 1861-62. and his friendship with Willie Lincoln. He titled the book *The Better Angels of Our Nature*, a line from Lincoln's 2nd inaugural speech.

He finally had the complete text of his manuscript ready on a CD-Rom, photographs on a DVD and written permission letters from sources ready to send to his publisher Adonis Press in San Francisco.

In the meantime he made reservations for May 21-28 on the California Zephyr train from Sacramento to Chicago and a connecting train south to Springfield, Illinois and return to Sacramento. Springfield is the site of the Lincoln Tomb, home, law office and brand new Lincoln Presidential Library & Museum. David made motel reservations at the Howard Johnson Motor Inn. The inn was conveniently located across the highway from Oak Ridge Cemetery and the Lincoln Tomb.

David's advance copy of the book arrived May 2nd just in time for his trip east to Springfield. Five of the copies he packed to be donated to the Abraham Presidential Library and researchers from the Illinois State Archives, Lincoln [public] Library and an independent researcher. [Unfortunately, some of the copies David received from the publisher were actually uncorrected proofs. In 2012 a second corrected edition was published].

After a sleepless night and day on the train (he couldn't afford the sleeping car prices that were three times coach) he arrived at the Springfield

Station on the evening of May 22, took a taxi to the motel and slept soundly till the next morning at 8 a.m.

Excited at the prospect of visiting the Lincoln Tomb, he hurriedly ate the complimentary continental breakfast of scrambled eggs, toast, cereal, OJ and coffee. He changed into his Pennsylvania 57th Regiment Union sergeant's replica uniform complete with kepi (cap) and went out into the brilliant warm sunshine blue sky Illinois prairie morning. He crossed the highway that had few cars for a workday week morning and walked along the grass bordering the the fence of the huge Oak Ridge Cemetery till he arrived at the side entrance.

He proceeded through the cemetery-- this part obviously newer with impressive monuments for World War I, II, Korea and Viet Nam.

He came around a curve and through the trees he saw the spire of the Lincoln Tomb standing majestically Oz-like at the end of a long green grass area with an Arch at the front of the main entrance to the Cemetery.

The tomb didn't open till 9 a.m. so David walked around to the rear of the edifice where he found the receiving vault where the president's and Willie's coffins (and later Eddie Lincoln's-- Eddie having died at 3-yrs-of-age in 1850 of TB before Willie was born) we're placed on May 4, 1865 till a permanent one could be built. On December 21, 1865 (ironically on what would have been Willie's fifteenth birthday) the coffins were moved from the receiving vault to a temporary underground vault. A small stone marker to the right of the tomb marked the spot. Visitors had left Lincoln cents on the bowl-shaped indentation on top of the marker and David did the same.

On July 15, 1871 Tad (Thomas) Lincoln died of "dropsy of the chest" (probably pleurisy that developed into pneumonia) at age eighteen. His coffin was added to the underground vault.

On July 16, 1882 (ironically almost eleven years to the day of Tad's death) Mary Todd Lincoln died and her coffin was placed next to Tad's, Willie's and Eddie's (in one) in the now completed permanent monumental tomb.

At 9 a.m. sharp the heavy door of the tomb opened and David along with a few other visitors entered. David signed the guest register and a tour-greeter pointed him to a hallway on the right that circled around to the actual tomb site. Sculptures of the president were set in carved niches on either side of the marble hallway.

The tomb itself was a rose-colored marble sarcophagus that actually is empty with the president's coffin ten feet below encased in a steel cement-filled frame to permanently discourage any attempt to steal Lincoln's body as had been attempted by counterfitters in the 1870s hoping to hold it for ransom.

Behind the sarcophagus in a circle were the flags of the states and District of Columbia where the president had lived and of course the US flag.

Where were the crypts of Willie and the others?

Almost immediately David felt that same sense of *presence* very near--the same thing he had experienced while writing the book-- as if *someone*--(Willie?) was hovering behind him as he wrote approving or disapproving of a particular line or phrase and silently but *authoritatively* communicated change but when he turned around of course there was no one there.

David then noticed the 11" x 14" ivy-garlanded (from the Carroll Tomb) enlargement (in an old 19th century oval frame he'd found in the attic) the last known photograph of Willie taken in April 1861 at Matthew Brady's Studio with Willie standing holding his Uncle Lockwood Todd's walking stick in his right hand. He felt that the eyes of the photo were staring right at him.

And now inside the Lincoln Tomb, the sense of *presence* was very strong and intimated to David to turn around. Inches from his back was Willie and Eddie's crypt:

Edward "Eddie" Baker
Lincoln
1846 - 1850
William "Willie" Wallace
Lincoln
1850 - 1862

David, oblivious to the other visitors listening to the elderly tour guide giving the history of the tomb, ran his fingers through the carved, marble letters of Willie's name praying and fighting back tears.

David stayed meditating at the crypt for awhile after the other visitors left then made his way around the left circular hall back to the lobby.

Crowding the lobby was a school class of boys appearing about 10-yrs-old, fifth-grade level. They stared, some smiling, at David in his Union sergeant's uniform. David saluted-- some saluted back.

He went back out into the May morning Illinois prairie sunshine, walked down the long grassy front area and took some photos of the tomb.

David called Walt back in Santa Losa and reported enthusiastically his mystical experience inside the Lincoln Tomb next to Willie's crypt saying, "I just left Willie! I mean his crypt." Then he walked back through the cemetery, crossed the highway and went to his room in the motor inn. He changed out of his replica Union uniform for the mile or so trek to downtown Springfield, first stopping on the way at a Subway restaurant for a 12" tuna fish, cheese, lettuce & tomato sub & chocolate milkshake-- needing lots of energy calories for the afternoon's pilgrimage to the Lincoln home site, law office, First Presbyterian Church (where the Lincoln family rented at pew-- the same as his great-greatfather had rented a pew in 1815 for $10 at the First Presbyterian Church in Lancaster, Pennsylvania after having immigrated from Ireland a few years earlier.) Unfortunately, the church was closed to visitors till June. David also would visit the Abraham Presidential Library & Museum.

David walked through the quiet, tree-lined Springfield streets, people of different nationalities nodding and saying friendly hellos.

It was about a mile to downtown and the first historical site he ran into was the restored train depot where Lincoln had given his farewell speech on February 11, 1861 before boarding the train for the long journey to Washington from which he would not return alive and neither would poor little Willie. There was a cast iron life-sized sculpture painted black of Lincoln sitting on a bench reading a newspaper something the future president must have done often in the years when he was just another Springfield citizen.

A few blocks away he came to the twin, sparkling new identical structures of the Abraham Lincoln Presidential Library and directly across the street the Abraham Lincoln Presidential Museum.

He stopped in the library first to give a copy of his book to a staff person then crossed the street to the museum.

After going through a security turnstile, he entered a large courtyard with life-sized manikins of the Lincoln family standing together in the center "greeting" all comers. David asked the museum guide to take a photo of him standing next to "Willie" and the family. Dioramas of different scenes in the life of the president surrounded the courtyard on three sides: Kentucky log cabin, Springfield home and White House.

On a side alcove a glass security box held the hair of Lincoln, Mary Todd and Willie. Across from it was another large enclosure which held the tombstone of Eddie Lincoln from old Hutchinson's Cemetery where he was interred in 1850.

It was late afternoon by the time he exited the museum after attending a holograph presentation of events in Lincoln's life and a play based on the recollections of several stage-hands who worked at Ford's Theatre before and after the assassination. They agonized on what, if anything, they could have done to stop that terrible event, but in the end accepted the fact that perhaps it was *fated* to happen.

He walked back to the motor inn cutting through the cemetery, ordered a Papa John's personal size pizza delivered sat back and watched the St. Louis Cardinals baseball game on TV-- the Cards being half the town's favorite and Chicago White Sox the other. Springfield was actually closer to St. Louis, Missouri (about a hundred miles) than Chicago. For some reason the Cubs didn't generate any interest in Southern Illinois.

The next day he stopped at the Lincoln Tomb Gift & Souvenir Shop just outside the main entrance of the cemetery and purchased postcards, a cap with "Springfield Land of Lincoln" printed on it, a dark-blue glass mug with different scenes in Lincoln's Springfield life on it and a T-shirt with President Obama's portrait on it in front of the Old State Calitol building.

David again walked downtown and found the Lincoln Home Site Visitors Cenrer and the home site itself and beautifully restored other bungalow-type homes of his neighbors. Even the street was unpaved gravel to give it authenticity (they couldn't leave it just dirt as it was in Lincoln's time as it would turn into mud).

David entered the home with a group and tour guide and found the rooms lovingly furnished with period pieces but was told the only original thing left of the interior structure (after a foolish renovation by an earlier private owner before the state took it over as a historic site) was the well-worn railing on the steps leading to the second floor. Even though thousands had touched the that railing over the past 150 years it was still moving to know that Lincoln, Willie and other family members had touched it.

Among the group touring the home was a mother and son from Missouri-- the mother chatted with David explaining her son was very "into" Willie and Tad. The boy, about ten, asked the tour guide if Willie and Tad had spilled ink on the floor of their bedroom as they had done while playing in Lincoln's Law Office. The tour guide said possibly, as there was a dark stain on the floor of the boys' bedroom they had all been looking into, David took a photo of the boy peering into the room.

There was a bench for weary tourists on the corner opposite the Lincoln home and David settled on it soon dozing off.

Awakening (*or was he still asleep*) the scene in front of the home appeared different. The Lincoln home that was freshly painted was now faded. A white picked fence surrounded the home and the street in front was a dusty-dirt. Most remarkable of all was the lack of the sound of automobile traffic a few streets away. Instead there was the clop-clop of horses' hooves on earth.

A solitary boy sat on the front step of the Lincoln home dressed in odd baggy brown clothes. He looked familiar.

David closed his eyes, opened them and the scene hadn't changed. The boy sitting on the steps, white picket fence, dirt street...

David thought, "If this is a dream, it's incredibly vivid!"

He walked slowly across the dirt street avoiding what looked like wagon wheel ruts and horse manure.

As he approached the house the boy on the steps stood up smiling, picked-up a sign that stated in carefully drawn but obviously a child's printing: **VOTE FOR OLD ABE.**

When he got close enough to see the boy's face, he recognized *who, impossibly*, he was looking at-- the bright-blue eyes, light-brown hair, with blond highlights, rather pale complexion was none other than Willie Lincoln!

Before he could stammer out a greeting-- shocked state he was in-- Willie broke the ice, "Good afternoon, sir. Do we have your vote for honest Abe?"

"Yes-- of course-- you-- you're the president's son-- I mean Mr. Lincoln's son, aren't you?"

Willie looked surprised for a minute, then said in a man-boy imitative tone trying to deepen his preadolescent high-pitched voice, "William Wallace Lincoln at your service, Sir, you said *president*-- I'm sure father will be elected but he was just nominated May 18."

"He WILL be, Willie-- do you mind if I sit down-- I'm a little lightheaded-- must be the heat."

"Of course, sir. Mother! Mrs. Vance! Could one of you please come out front for a minute?"

A minute later the front door opened and a Black woman [Mrs. Marian Vance, the Lincoln housekeeper 1850-60] said, "Willie-- what in tarnation are you yellin' 'bout?" Then seeing David sitting next to Willie, "Oh! beg yr' pardon sir-- didn't know Willie had company."

"Mrs. Vance-- this is Mr.-- what is your name sir?"

"David Platon."

"David is a bit hot and thirsty. Could you bring us some of your delicious lemonade please?"

"Why, sure Willie-- be back in a minute."

While waiting for the lemonade Willie chattered on about the excitement in town-- parades, bands, bonfires-- since his father's nomination a week ago.

"Willie, forgive me-- it must be the heat and my long travel-- but what is the date?"

"Why May 26, sir," Willie said, looking concerned.

"What year?"

"1860," Willie replied and then the lemonade arrived and Willie added, "You better drink this sir."

David drank deeply. It was the best he'd ever tasted. Even the air although hot, *tasted good*--fresh.

"David, if you don't mind me asking where are you from. Your clothes are different."

"From California." David had on jeans, a beige safari-type jacket with four front pockets, two of which held his digital camera and cell phone, and comfortable desert boots.

"That sure must have been a long trip-- over the mountains and deserts," Willie said, impressed.

"It was tiring but the scenery was beautiful."

"Did you see and buffalo and wild Indians?"

"Yes," David fibbed-- and lots of elk," which was true.

Something was beginning to change. The light was beginning to fade taking on a sepia hue like an old photograph.

David stood up, backed away a few feet from the steps and reached in his pocket and brought out his digital camera and quickly snapped a photo of Willie who quickly asked, "What was that?"

"It's a miniature camera-- a new invention in California. I'm trying it out. If it comes out OK, I'll mail you a copy," David explained.

"Well Willie I'd better be going. It was GREAT meeting you. Please tell your father he IS going to be president." He wanted to give the boy a hug but instead held out his hand which Willie shook vigorously.

"Maybe I'll see you *again*, David."

"Maybe-- *anything* is possible."

As he walked away darkness swept over him and he awoke on the bench back in 2009.

That was so real-- but I must have been dreaming, he thought. Then he felt something brushing his leg on the bench. It was a half-empty glass of lemonade.

David got up and began the long walk back to the motor inn.

He took the motor inn courtesy van to the train station the next morning expecting to catch the 10:15 Texas Star coming from St. Louis through to Chicago but was told by the ticket booth attendant there had been an accident in Texas and a man had been run over and killed by the train delaying its arrival by four hours.

However, Amtrak had arranged for a motor coach (tour bus) to take the passengers to Chicago in time to make their connecting trains. It was a pleasant trip through the flat prairie Illinois countryside. Farms, small towns and occasional patches of old-growth woods stood out like sentries. The highway even went through Lincoln, Illinois.

They made Union Station in Chicago with an hour to spare.

He caught the California Zephyr back to Sacramento where Walt picked him up at the station and drove him home to Santa Losa.

16.

David had mixed feelings-- pride and a sense of accomplishment but also an *emptyness.* He had completed the book he had worked hard on for five and a half years. It had been published, he'd taken the pilgrimage to Georgetown and Springfield he'd dreamed about for years while on incarcerated sabbatical yet felt a kind of literary postpartum depression. David wondered if other writers felt a similar sense of loss once the labor, birthing and publishing had occurred?

David decided that it was the *journey* of the actual writing that was the greatest reward.

17.

Lonelyhood.

Dolores had been the only new person in his life he'd told about his past and listing on the digital scarlet letter Megan's Law Sex Offender Register because her daughter had married a sex offender and she was empathic.

He was reluctant to tell other new acquaintances for fear of the sex panic knee jerk reaction rejection that was fueled by the myths fed to the public by the media and politicians ignoring the fact that sex offenders have a very LOW recidivism rate-- actually only 5.3% in three years according to a recent study done by the U.S. Department of Justice and the Department of Corrections.

Loneliness.

Fear of rejection.

Isolation.

A pariah.

These were temporarily assuaged by *movement--* physical and intellectual. If he sat around thinking about and dwelling on his situation depression and atrophy would set in. He fought against it by writing in his study or researching online at the north branch of the Santa Losa Public Library six mornings a week. On Sunday mornings he relaxed reading the newspaper and watching his favorite news program "This Week With George Stephanopolous."

Afternoons he would walk along the Wapinoma River Path the 2.3 mile 33 block walk from his house to center city. Then have lunch at the

Raspberry Square Food Court, walk over to City Island and attend a Santa Losa Indians minor league baseball game if the team was home and then walk back home on the river path. The sun-sparkling water, that the Native American Wampinoma tribe called *kipona*, the cool breeze, florid groves along the way, passersby walking, jogging and bicycling all raised his spirits and made him feel a part of *something greater* and arriving back at his house he felt a sated, peaceful contentment,

Then David would make dinner, watch the six-o'clock news, read a literary novel, watch PBS and retire early only to wake early often before dawn when the cold clarity of reality would confront him and he would moan *I'm alone and probably always will be.*

18.

Sunday, June 30, 2009.

A gray, cloudy day, warm with a threat of showers.

The Indians were playing on City Island at 1 O'clock so David did his fast fifty minute walk along the river path to city center, crossed the old (1899) iron suspension bridge nicknamed the "singing bridge" because when the wind blew hard enough the swaying produced a whistling sound.

The bridge had originally been open to vehicular traffic but a spring storm and flood in '95 had knocked over the western extension leading to several small communities that never had enough funds to build a new structure. The remaining side was repaired and opened to pedestrian and bicycle traffic.

He purchased his ticket for $5 and made his way up to the stands on the third base side where he usually sat.

Before the start of the game an announcement was made that the former major league player Tommy Davis was signing free autographs at a booth behind the stands. Davis had starred for the Giants in the early '60s and David collected baseball memorabilia so he asked a gentleman seated near him to save his seat and placed his water bottle there.

He bought an Indians team baseball at the souvenir shop and got in line for the autograph. Davis was very friendly and gracious and seemed genuinely flattered that fans still remember him from his playing days.

"Not too many people remember me-- I really appreciate it," When David had complimented him on his play.

When he returned to his seat he found it occupied by a young woman and young boy. David remarked that he had been sitting there and the woman apologized and she and her son (he would soon learn) scooted over. The boy sat between David and his mother. David retrieved his water bottle that had been moved.

The boy asked how David got the autographed ball. David explained. He asked his mom could he get one too but mom, an attractive athletic-looking brunette with striking blue eyes, “Maybe later, Tommy.”

The woman introduced herself as Mary and her son Tommy. Mary appeared to be in her early 30s. David then introduced himself.

Both Mary and Tommy were very friendly and talkative. Mary explained that Tommy played soccer but didn’t know much about baseball and wanted to learn. David was a little surprised that the boy “didn’t know much about baseball” being America’s pass time at his age (he was eight). Mary said she played soccer and softball in college and worked summers in concessions at Giants baseball games while attending the University of San Francisco.

Mary also remarked she had a friend who played for the Santa Losa Indians a few seasons ago named Hosea Mirez.

David and Mary took turns explaining various plays happening on the field and rules of the game.

Then David noticed she was wearing a T-shirt with St. Mark’s Methodist School printed on it.

David inquired about the church itself and Mary replied that it was progressive with a diverse congregation that included African-American, Hispanic and Gay members and added that the church school that she was a trustee of, was also diverse and included minorities and others on scholarships, students didn’t have to be a member of the church next door and it had a high academic rating.

David had been thinking of attending a church but understandably had reservations about how and when to reveal his past a an (s)ex offender registered on the Megan’s Law website where even supposedly loving Christian congregations who were suppose to follow Jesus’s maxims of *Ye without sin cast the first stone* and *judge ye not; lest ye be judged thyself* but he feared, as he had heard, that he would be profiled, stereotyped as a social pariah.

The loneliness, isolation and fear of rejection was always with him. He imagined the Megan's Law registration hung on him in a bright scarlet lettered sign:

SEXUAL PREDATOR - BEWARE

However, for those few hours on that gray, dreary Sunday afternoon in June 2009 with Mary and Tommy he felt like a member of the community and accepted. He allowed himself the harmless fantasy that *Mary was his daughter and Tommy his grandson--* both which he would never have.

Mary excused herself and took Tommy down to the concession stand to get something to eat. Mary came back with a beer, Tommy with a bottle of water and slice of pizza.

David then excused himself and went down, used the restroom and bought a "Indian dog"-- an inexpensive ballpark hot dog.

When David returned Tommy exclaimed, "That looks good! Can I get one mom?"

"Later, honey-- eat your pizza for now."

David noticed that Mary was wearing a Giants baseball hat and he himself was wearing an Indians one but little Tommy was bareheaded. David excused himself once more and went to the souvenir stand and bought Tommy an Indians hat.

David brought the hat up to his seat and placed on Tommy's head.

"Did you buy that for Tommy?"

"Yes, it's just a random act of kindness Tommy-- pay it forward. Tomorrow do something nice for somebody."

"Yes, Tommy, pay it forward," Mary said as she adjusted the strap on David's hat so it fit snug.

"Thank you so much David!" Tommy said.

"You're quite welcome," David said and patted Tommy on the back.

Mary, looking serious, said to David, "He lost his grandfather recently."

"I'm sorry, Mary." David said, suspecting that it was her father that had died.

The first game (it was a doubleheader) was over and threatening to rain and David had the fifty-minute walk home.

Before David left he asked Mary if he could take their photo for "posterity" he explained. Mary said sure. David said, "It was very nice to meet you both," and added, "If I don't see you before your birthday (it was in August) have a happy birthday Tommy."

"It was very nice to meet you, too, and thank you for your kindness to Tommy."

During the walk home David scarcely noticed the drizzle that had begun about 20th Street. He held is his thoughts the heart-warming fantasy of mother and son being his daughter and grandson. Although it had only been a few hours of socializing at a baseball game, the kindness of strangers had made him happy and forget his pariahdom-- and for that he was eternally grateful.

19.

Rash moment?

Over the 4th of July weekend David attended the three-day festival along river front and on City Island that included Santa Losa Indians baseball games and fireworks after Friday night's game.

He thought often of Mary and Tommy and hoped he would run into them again.

He had the photo of Mary and Tommy he had taken and it was a beautiful spontaneous portrait of the two. If he had the foresight to have asked for Mary's e-mail address he would have sent her a copy.

He carried a copy of the photo with him all three days of the festival--scanning the crowds but never saw them again.

About two weeks later on Thursday, July 18 about noon David was walking along river front and noticed the red door of St. Mark's Methodist Church standing open. He crossed the street and saw a sign stating "Thursday Worship Service 12:00".

Mary had mentioned the congregation was liberal and diverse and David had been looking for a church for some time but had hesitated because of the sex panic reaction of his digital scarlet letter Megan's Law registration being revealed with inevitable rejection.

He also wondered if Mary and Tommy attended the church, or just the school next door-- she hadn't said.

David entered and unconsciously signed his pen name, David Espoir in the visitor's book in the vestibule.

There were only a few elderly people in the church. A white-haired woman in her 70s approached him smiling. She introduced herself as Dorothy Freund and asked if she could help him. David said he was passing by and was curious about the church and had met some people at a Santa Losa Indians baseball game about two weeks ago who said the church had a diverse congregation and that he had recently returned to the area and was looking for a church to attend. Dorothy asked who the people were. David replied that he only knew their first names-- Mary and her son Tommy. Dorothy immediately recognized them as Mary and Tommy Simmerson and said they were wonderful people and although they didn't attend the church, Mary was very active as a trustee of the school next door that Tommy attended.

David stayed for the service and was invited back for the following Sunday's service.

David had been working on his 12th book *The Better Angels of Our Nature* for four and a half years and while excitedly waiting for the book's release on August 3rd, was promoting it by identifying himself by his pen name Daniel Espoir much as Samuel Clemens identified himself as Mark Twain did when promoting his books. David was not trying to deceive anyone since many people in Santa Losa knew who he was and he had been using his pen name since the early 1970s.

David attended the service the following Sunday with a friend from college Barbara Trator who was visiting from Oakland. They had been in the same Advance Composition Class with the esteemed poet Dr. Carl Patchin. Patchin had "discovered" David's budding talent for writing (poetry at the time) in 1969 and they remained friends after David's graduation in 1970 and after Patchin's retirement in 1985. The last time David had visited Patchin had informed he had terminal throat cancer (he smoked like a chimney for years). That was in the fall of 1991. In the spring issue of the *Berkeley Alumni Quarterly* he read that Dr. Patchin had died in April 1992 and interment was to be in Riverview Cemetery in his hometown of San Loquia. David visited the cemetery but although he found Patchin's parents graves, he could not find the professor's. So David placed an entry in "Gravesend", a website for those looking for graves of relatives and friends.

Years had passed and one day in July 2009 David received an e-mail from Barbara stating she could show him the grave of Dr. Patchin if he could meet her there the following Sunday at 1 p.m. They met as scheduled and Barbara took him to a spot behind the graves of Patchin's parents and pointed to a plot of grass where she said she believed the cremated remains in an urn were buried. She said there had been a small tin temporary marker like those given by funeral homes. They searched around and finally found the marker bent, rusted and half-buried behind the gravestone of his parents. David dug it out straightened it as best he could and wiped it off with a rag from the trunk of his car. David read a poem he had written for Dr. Patchin who had only been 68 when he went into the great mystery--death. David and Barbara both placed flowers at the site.

David and Barbara started dating alternating between her home in Oakland and David's in Santa Losa. She confessed that she had an affair with Dr. Patchin after he had separated from his wife and had taken care of him during his illness.

One Sunday, July 21 David and Barbara entered St. Mark's and she signed the guest book. They took a seat in the rear of the church. Barbara seemed uncomfortable-- said she really had issues with organized religion and only attended this time as a courtesy to David. Barbara didn't participate in the hymn singing or prayers. She got up and went outside to River Front Park to wait for David when the service was finished.

After the service as people were exiting Dorothy introduced him to various members of the congregation.

When David met Barbara who had been sitting on a bench enjoying the view of river, she apologized but stressed she didn't believe in God and felt *in-authentic* attending a ritual worshipping a God she didn't believe in. David didn't pursue the issue.

David returned for the following Thursday's service and while sitting with Dorothy and her husband mentioned the photo he had taken of Mary and Tommy at the baseball game that turned out so well and said he'd bring it along for her to give to Mary (they were good friends) sometime. David repeated how impressed he was with the two.

Dorothy said Tommy was a very special boy-- empathic beyond his years (he was eight) and that he had been known to give his lunch money to the homeless people that frequented River Front Park across Front Street from the church and school while his class was in the park in nice weather to eat their lunches.

The following Sunday David again walked to St. Marks' in the July morning heat wearing his suit and tie even though formal dressing for church was optional now days unlike when David was growing up in the 1950s and '60s. Some people were even in T-shirts and jeans.

He sat with Dorothy and her husband Frank, a retired banker, as he had the previous Sunday. After the service, which he enjoyed, he passed out a few of the business cards he had printed promoting his new book and introduced himself as Daniel Espoir.

David had filled out a card requesting a "home visit" by one of the pastors at the church to discuss his interest perhaps joining the church and of course explaining about his past.

Unfortunately, Rev. Marcade, who did the home visits was on vacation for two weeks but David was told he would be put on the waiting list.

This situation would have unforeseen consequences for David.

David was introduced to more congregation members on the steps as he was exiting-- this time by Reverend Clement, whom he had met along with Dorothy that first Thursday he had walked through the red door.

David, genuinely moved (naively as he would soon learn) said, "I feel I've found a spiritual home-- I've come *home.*"

Dorothy and her husband even gave David a ride home.

20.

Digital scarlet letter shock.

The following Thursday David attended the service as usual and brought along the photo of Mary and Tommy he had taken at the baseball game to give to Dorothy to give to Mary when she next saw her.

As usual there were only a few loyal members of the congregation present-- and of course Dorothy and Reverend Clement.

Before the start of the service David brought out the photo and showed it to Dorothy.

"It's a wonderful likeness of both," Dorothy said.

"In appreciation for their friendliness and kindness to me at the game, would you please give it to Mary when you see her."

"Of course-- that probably won't be till September when school starts."

"That's fine since I don't expect to see her again," David replied.

In the middle of the service during a prayer David noticed Rev. Clement leave the pulpit and go out a side door. He came back a moment later-- a solemn expression on his face and approached David.

"David, someone would like to speak to you outside for a moment."

David, curious and somewhat alarmed at *who* was out there and *what* they might want. David followed Clement through the side door that lead to a passageway between the church and the school next door.

David was shocked to see a uniformed Santa Rosa policeman standing there.

"Hello, I'm Sgt. Jackson-- do you have identification with you?"

David said yes and took out his driver's license and handed it to the officer.

"You are David Platon?"

"Yes."

"We received a complaint from a member of the congregation that you are listed on the Megan's Law website and have been attending services-- is that correct?"

"Yes-- I enjoy them very much."

"Are you on probation or parole?"

"No-- I maxed out from Shanksville June 11, 2008."

Jackson then got on his walkie-talkie and called headquarters confirming what David had said.

"Well, members of the church are not *comfortable* with your attending services," Jackson said.

"In that case-- I sure don't want to make anyone uncomfortable-- I'll leave-- however, I'd like to finish the service-- it's almost over," David said and went back inside.

Dorothy asked, looking concerned, "What's wrong?"

"A misunderstanding," David replied.

A few minutes later David was called back outside.

"You are in violation of Megan's Law because of the school next door," Jackson said accusingly.

"Actually, thats not accurate-- Act 83 states that sex offenders on probation or parole cannot live within 1,500 feet of a school. I am NOT on either. Furthermore, the school doesn't even open till September and I would have only been attending Sunday services," David said, irritated by the officer's ignorance of the law.

"Also, you passed out cards listing an alias, Daniel Espoir, and signed the visiting book with that alias-- that shows *deception*."

"That's my pen name-- I have a book coming out August 3-- I wasn't trying to deceive anyone. Just like Samuel Clemens used Mark Twain when promoting one of his books that was about to be released," David retorted, visibly upset.

The officer looking a bit perplexed, as if not sure what to say next, said, "Well, what are you going to do?"

"I'll leave-- I'll find a church that's not judgmental about my past..."

Dorothy, who had followed Rev. Clement outside asked, "Do you want me to give the picture to Tommy?"

"NO-- I'll take care of it," David said as he walked away deeply hurt and angry.

Later he discovered that Dorothy had misunderstood thinking David would try to contact Tommy (actually) Mary and give her the photo himself which he had no intention of doing.

21.

A CARDIAC ARREST.

After leaving St. Mark's that fateful Thursday, David, now more angry than in shock, walked rapidly over the bridge to City Island. He hesitated in front of a trash can at the end of the bridge debating whether to throw the photo away.

"No, why should I," He said out loud resulting in the curious looks from passersby.

"I didn't do anything wrong-- I had no inappropriate fantasies about Tommy-- only the loneliness-born fantasy of Tommy being his grandson and Mary his daughter-- his adult ADHD afflicted son had produced two daughters out of wedlock-- one given up for adoption," David self-talked as he walked around the island.

His anger was not just at whoever in the congregation looked up David on the Megan's Law website and immediately had the typical sex panic knee-jerk reaction thinking the worst just because he wanted to give a photo of a mother and son to them out of gratitude for the kindness to him, but also to Rev. Clement who may have been the one who looked him up [later confirmed] for not at least sitting down with him before calling the neo-Nazi sexual police. David's fears of being stereotyped and profiled based on false rates of recidivism (actually only 5.3%) had become a reality.

David was also angry at himself for his rash moment trusting and longing to belong, naivete and stupidity on one hand and a kind of pride in the upcoming publication of his book using his pen name to identify himself blinding him to the reality of people's reactions.

What did the Bible say: *Pride goeth before destruction and a haughty spirit before a fall.*

A month went by and David heard nothing more from the police, never went back to St. Mark's, never tried to contact Mary.

He did feel bad about Dorothy who had been welcoming (before the discovery of his digital scarlet letter listing) so he looked up her address in the phone book and again-- thinking cardiacally rather than rationally, wrote to her-- explaining he was deeply saddened and hurt by the knee jerk stereotyping reaction to his digital scarlet letter listing and the fact that David's *offense* was twelve years ago. He stated the general circumstances that led to it-- the death of his parents within ten months of each other and the death of an adored pet and suicide of a close friend all culminating in a slow spiral downward to depression and despair and his fateful meeting Blonde at the North Santa Losa Swim Club Pool in 1997. He stressed his years of group and individual counseling and his NEVER permitting inappropriate fantasies ever again. The thought that someone would assume that he would harm Tommy in any way disgusted him and he reiterated the fact that he only wanted to repay their kindness with a gift of the excellent photo. He stated that Dorothy was a "true Christian" and that some others in the church were pseudo-Christians because of their ignorant judgmentalism and NOT following Jesus's maxims: *Judge ye not, lest ye be judged* and *If any of you be without sin, cast the first stone* and instead rejected outright his participation in church.

He ended the letter inviting her to meet at some public place to discuss his situation and enclosed a copy of his book *The Better Angels of Our Nature* and the photo of Mary and Tommy to give to them.

Dorothy wrote back thanking him for the book and photo and said they could meet at Murphy's Restaurant and 2nd and Vernova Sts. some morning, a stop she always made before heading to St. Mark's. She said she would let him know.

Two more weeks passed.

Rash moment number three?

David phoned Dorothy one evening and asked if they could meet that week. Sounding nervous, "No-- I'm busy-- I'll let you know."

"Have you given the photo to Mary yet?"

"No-- I have company-- must go now, goodby."

22.

Friday, September 6, 2009

THE CARDIAC ARREST.

About 1:20 p.m. there was a loud knocking on David's front door.

David peered out through the blinds and saw two husky, suited men.

His heart sank-- beating furiously.

David opened the door asking, "May I help you?"

They showed their Santa Losa Police badges and the older of the two identified himself as Detective Ralph Hellner and asked if they could come in.

David said, "Sure," and let them in.

Hellner explained that he was responsible for monitoring the 121 sex offenders living within the city limits and likes to get to know them.

A few minutes later another car pulled up (unmarked as was Hellner and his buddy's. The man who got out David recognized as the man who had registered him at the State Police barracks back in June 2008.

He came in the house and said to David, "I have to take you into custody for violation of Megan's Law registration requirements," (without reading him his Miranda rights) and asked him to turn around. He was then handcuffed. Hellner seemed surprised and asked the state policeman, "Are you sure about this?"

"The D.A approved it."

"Do you want me to take him to city hall lockup?" Hellner asked.

"No, since this is a state charge, I'll take him to the barracks first to process him and then the district justice."

David, in deep shock, nauseated and near tears, managed to stammer, "WHAT did I do?"

"You didn't list your *alias* at registration-- a felony."

David was marched out to the state policeman's car, placed in the front seat and driven to the state police barracks several miles east of Santa Losa. He was fingerprinted, photographed and the officer asked if *now* he wanted to list his *alias.*

David replied, "Yes-- but I never thought of my pen name as an alias-- I've used it since the 1970s on my books-- NOT for any criminal purposes..."

The officer did not reply to this but said, "Now I have to take you to the J.P (Justice of the Peace) for bail to be set."

Bail was set at $25,000 secured. He was allowed a phone call and fortunately Walt was home.

"Walt, I'm in a situation here. I need you to go up to my house and get my checkbook, call a bailbond's man and and ask him to meet you at Condor County Prison ASAP."

David was transported to CCP where he waited for hours till Walt showed up with the bailbonds man about 9 p.m.. He was released and wrote a check for the bailbond's man. Walt took him home and on the way he explained what they both thought was a ridiculous charge.

One good thing-- the JP hadn't put any restrictions on David while he was out on bail. After all he hadn't victimized anyone but *himself.*

Walt commented, "I had trouble finding a bailbonds man-- they said they wouldn't *touch* a Megan's Law case--finally found that guy in Sacramento."

"Another example of stereotyping-- I don't even have a *victim*," David replied.

23.

After a sleepless night David called his old attorney Jim Donkle, a decision he'd later regret-- briefly explained the situation of his oversight of not listing his pen name as a so called *alias* at the Megan's Law registration. David asked Donkle if he'd represent him at the preliminary hearing set for next Thursday at 9 a.m. at the J.P.

Donkle told him to come to his office the next day at 9 a.m.

Donkle's office looked the same as it had eleven years prior-- dusty, piles of papers everywhere.

David went through his story. After he was done, Donkle said, "Well, since you didn't do anything to the boy, it looks like they're going after you 'cause you didn't list your *nom de plume* as an alias."

"It was an oversight-- never thought of my pen name as an alias-- never used it for anything illegal," David said vehemently.

"I agree-- but they're looking at it as if you were trying to get to the boy-- they take this stuff very seriously."

Donkle picked up David Thursday morning and took him to the hearing. Once inside, David told him to wait while he went into the hearing room to talk to the judge, D.A.'s representative.

While David was waiting, Rev. Clement and Dorothy came in and went into the hearing room.

After a few minutes, Clement, Dorothy and a young woman who turned out to be an assistant D.A. came out of the hearing room and went outside. A few minutes later the assistant D.A. came back in and went into the hearing room. Clement and Dorothy left in an SUV.

Donkle came out and asked David if he agreed not to contact Dorothy anymore. David said of course-- he had no intention of doing that.

"Alright, let's go in," Donkle said.

The only people there in addition to David and his attorney were the assistant D.A, the arresting state policeman and the judge.

Donkle whispered to David that a witness failed to show up and the prosecution wanted to waive the hearing and for David to sign papers agreeing to waive the hearing and they'd be on their way.

David, naive and ignorant about the legal process, and trusting his attorney (stupidly) signed the papers-- not knowing at the time that a rule of court procedure guaranteed his right to a fair and impartial hearing to confront his accuser and the prosecution CANNOT waive without the accused's consent and must reschedule.

Donkle and the D.A had conspired to get him to sign the waiver papers stating that HE, David, waived the hearing and was not advised of the fact that he could refuse.

As he and Donkle were about to leave, Ralph Hellner, the missing witness for the prosecution pulled up in his Dakota truck, smiled at David through his windshield and went in the J.P.'s office.

On the way back David asked to see the sentencing guidelines for his supposed offense *Failure to give accurate information, sex offender registration* (failure to list his pen name as an alias).

"I can't figure this out?" David asked.

"Well, initially I thought it was a county sentence, 9-18 months but in 2008 the D.A.'s Association and the state legislature got together and concocted an enhancement of the offense to a felony punishable by 5-10 yrs. Evidently, they snuck it in with an unrelated Bill 179," Donkle explained.

David, shocked, said, "That's as much as some sex offenses themselves!"

"I know-- but I can't so anything about it."

"I guess I'm up shit-creek without a paddle!."

"Pretty much."

Nothing more was said until Donkle dropped him off at his house.

"You'll get a notice in the mail for the date of the arraignment-- meet me at my office a half hour before the time designated."

At the arraignment the following week David pleaded not guilty, signed more papers and was told he'd be notified by mail of the trial date. David's attorney obtained three continuances over the following months October through December 2009.

24.

In those same months David continued to see Barbara Trator, mostly taking the hour train ride to Oakland from Santa Losa. Barbara would pick him up and take her to her small duplex in the Oakland suburbs. The front of the house was nearly obscured by trees and bushes but the backyard was large-- sloping down to a towpath that encircled the development. There was a nice view of woods and farmland beyond.

The interior of the house was problematic-- at least by David's standards of cleanliness and order. Three cats roamed the premises, shedding fur everywhere. The eldest was arthritic and had trouble making it on time to her litter box (the other two felines had their own). The elder cat's litter box was currently placed in a corner of the kitchen, odoriferously conflicting with the appetizing odors of her scrumptious cooking. She seemed to enjoy preparing delicious meals for David when he spent weekends visiting. Barbara loved to drive and she delighted in taking David on scenic rides all over the county in her Subaru and taking him hiking on lost Indian trails and logging paths in the foothills of the Sierra Nevadas.

They had shared eclectic literary interests as David discovered obscure classics such as *Wisconsin Death Trip, The Lost Boys: James Barrie and the Llewelyn-Davies Boys* and *Les Amitiés Particulierés (Special Friendships)* in her library in the small and clean (compared to the other rooms) comfy living room. Although she read widely her personal talent was art-- drawing and painting. David thought she was quite good but he was not an art critic.

On the few occasions after the Sunday she had attended St. Mark's with David she had also accompanied him to Santa Losa Indians baseball games-- saying her father had got her interested in the San Francisco Giants and went to games with him as a young girl.

On a bright August Sunday afternoon they had walked over the bridge to City Island and taken a ride on the Pride of the Wampinoma-- a small version of a Mississippi River steamboat.

As he became friendlier with Barbara, he wrestled with when to tell her of his past, listing on the Megan's Law website. He finally decided to break the news on a weekday afternoon in late August on the campus of Berkeley-- on the occasion of a sentimental return to their alma mater.

"Twelve years ago I did something stupid. I was in a pretty deep depression after the deaths of both my parents within ten months of each other at ages 80 and 81, my pet cat at 16½ and a dear friend to suicide at 35. In 1997 I met this beautiful blond boy at a swimming pool and fell in love with him as he did me. Unfortunately, he was under the legal age of consent in this country. Someone suspected and called the neo-Nazi sexual police and when they interviewed him they lied to him saying I confessed and Jamie, that was his name, felt betrayed and confessed. I spent time in prison and I'm listed on the Megan's Law website. If you don't want anything more to do with me, I'll understand."

"I didn't expect anything like this-- I kinda' feel sick to my stomach-- but I appreciate your honesty and yes, we can still be friends."

David was relieved as he hoped to gain at least one new friend who wouldn't reject him as a pariah.

"Something else Barbara-- I don't go to St. Mark's any more. Someone, I suspect that Rev. Clement, checked online and found me on the Megan's Law website, freaked-out with a typical ignorant sex panic knee-jerk panicky reaction, and without even discussing it with me, called the Santa Losa Police who showed up at the last Thursday service I attended, had me called outside of the church and said some of the congregation weren't *comfortable* with my attending. The cop also accused me of deception because I used my pen name on a few business cards I passed out and identified myself by my pen name but that was only to promote my book (as you know) *The Better Angels of Our Nature* that was being released August 3, the same as Samuel Clemens used his pen name Mark Twain when one of his tomes was being published. Anyhow, I told Clement I wouldn't be comfortable with them either and I left. I wrote a letter to the church saying they were pseudo-Christians and Jesus wouldn't have rejected me. Fuckin' hypocrites-- don't you think?"

"Yes, I don't have anything to with those superstitious phonies-- only went along with you that day as a favor-- I was very uncomfortable in that building," Barbara said.

25.

One humid day in late August David was waiting for the #6 bus in City Square to go back home as it was too hot to take his usual 2½ mile trek home and noticed a man and his young son asking people in broken English what # bus went to Valentia, the town directly south of Santa Losa. They didn't seemed to be getting understood and looked somewhat desperate. The young boy, pale and thin looking about eight, smiled at David (kid magnet that David had experienced since he was 14) and walked right over to him. The boy asked in an accent, but understandable, "Please sir- what number bus to Valentia?"

"Why, #19 son."

David followed the boy who told his dad (who looked immeasurably relieved) pointing to David.

David showed the father the printed bus schedule for the #19 to Valentia that was pasted on the inside of the Plexiglass window of the enclosed waiting shelter. Both father and son thanked David profusely.

A few days later David was taking a short cut home through beautiful, florid Mexican Lake Park and ran into a family sitting on a blanket enjoying the nice day. He immediately recognized the father and son from the bus stop. Accompanying them was a woman, presumably the mother and two small girls likely the boy's younger sisters.

The boy recognizing David, smiled and said to his dad, "Father it's the man from the bus stop!"

The following Saturday, a rainy, humid morning, David was walking to the north branch of the Santa Losa Library and noticed a well-dressed family of five waiting in the #3 bus shelter. When he got closer he recognized the family from the park.

"Hello again," David said.

"It's nice to see you again," the father said-- the rest of the family smiling along with him,

"May I ask where you're from?" David asked.

"We're from Afghanistan-- we've only been here a week,"

"Welcome to America! If I can be of assistance to you in any way, let me know. My name is Dave," David said and offered his hand which the father shook firmly.

"You can call me Bill-- it's easier to remember," he said and introduced the rest of the family-- his wife Amira, son Hassan and daughters Minaya and Sareya.

David asked if Hassan liked sports.

"Yes, what you call soccer, of course, but he wants to learn how to play American football and baseball, too," Bill replied.

"Well, maybe I'll see you again," David said as the family's bus arrived.

David realized they must be going to attend Saturday Islamic services at the local Mosque in Valentia.

By the middle of the next week the rainy, humid low finally moved away and more typical breezy sunny days returned.

A few days later David had taken his typical walk back home and walked through the Riverview apartment complex a few blocks from his house when he saw Hassan kicking a soccer ball around in front of one of the units.

Hassan, spying David, ran smiling up to him and said, "We live on 2nd floor there. Come see father. Maybe you teach me baseball?" He continued, grinning hopefully.

"We'll see-- I'll ask your dad," David replied as Bill came out the door of the building after Hassan's exuberant calls for his father.

David shook hands with Bill again and they exchanged pleasantries-- Hassan interjecting entreaties about baseball.

Labor Day September 6th arrived and like July 4th a three-day celebration that included a variety of music groups performing, ethnic foods, kids' rides, boat races on the Wapinoma and Indians baseball games on City

Island. The annual event drew thousands from the city and surrounding communities.

At Indians games they always had promotional giveaways for the kids on a first-come basis. The afternoon game on the 5th the giveaway was a baseball with the Indians logo on it.

On the walk back home after the game David had the idea that Hassan would like the baseball and David had one of clairvoyant-precognitive-coinciding-synchronistic episodes where he *saw* himself running smack into Hassan and giving him the baseball. This episode came into his consciousness out of the blue (as they always did) about halfway-home on the river front path.

Twenty minutes later he came to the edge of the apartment complex that ran for four blocks north on 30th Street. About two blocks in he saw the figure of a boy walking toward him on the same side of the street. As he got closer he was surprised (but not much) to see little Hassan was the boy. He was playing with a toy twirling colored plastic hoops with a plastic stick.

When they met David said, "Do you remember me?"

"Sure-- Dave!"

"Would you like a baseball?"

"Yes! Thank you-- come and show father!"

Hassan ran ahead excitedly and David followed to the the front of the family's apartment about two blocks away.

Hassan ran into the building, which was a two-story with first and second floor apartments. Hassan ran up the steps to his 2nd floor apartment, dropping the ball in his youthful exuberance. The ball bounced down the steps and out the door where David retrieved it and gave it to Hassan as he came bounding back down the steps followed by his Dad Bill.

"Hi, Bill. I ran into Hassan on my way back from a Santa Losa Indians baseball game on City Island. They gave baseballs away before the game as a promotion and running into Hassan I thought he might like it."

Hassan then said, "Father, you can get me a bat and glove and we can play!"

"We'll see," Bill replied.

"That was the last game of the season-- maybe we could all go to a game next season," David said.

"If we're still here in a year. I may be going back to Afghanistan once I get my family settled."

Bill went on to explain that he learned English at the American School in Kabul, went to Kabul University and graduated with a degree in business and had a good job but lost it when the Taliban attacked and America invaded. He got a job driving a truck to support his family. He said they lived in a middle-class northern section of Kabul near his parents. Then when the American army came into the city he got a job as an interpreter for the Army. An errant rocket fired by unknown parties hit his father's house killing him. Thankfully, his mother was not home at the time. She then went to live with Bill and his family. She decided to stay in Kabul when the family left Afghanistan saying, "I was born here, my husband died her, my children and grandchildren were born here and here I shall die." The final straw that prompted their move to America came one day as Bill was walking home from his job as an interpreter. About a block from his house he heard a loud explosion. The ground shook and windows in nearby homes and shops shattered. He ran toward his house as fast as he could. When he arrived he saw that a neighbor's house at the far end of the block was now a hole of smoldering ruins. A few torn bodies lay in the street. At that moment he saw Hassan and Minaya coming out of Ali's Grocery Store and rushed to them.

"Are you two alright," Bill said to the terrified, crying children.

"Yes, Father, we were inside the store," Hassan said, drying tears staining his face.

"Mr. Binhari and his young daughter were killed along with four other passersby. It was a miracle my children were not hurt. Soon after, with the help of the American Army, we were able to get a sponsor through the American Afghan Association, flew initially to Switzerland then to New York city, then here. Now my children can safely get an education. The only problem I'm having is finding work."

The U.S. economy is bad right now-- in a mild recession. I hope President Obama can do something to stimulate the economy and create more jobs," David explained.

About two weeks later Barbara came to visit on a Sunday and I asked if she would like to meet my friends the Afghan family.

It was a bright-blue and gold October day as they walked through Mexican Lake Park, continued on to 30th Street to the front of the Afghan's family unit. Hassan and Minaya were kicking around a soccer ball in the long green lawn in front.

Hassan saw David and ran up to him smiling and said, "Hi!" Bill came down the stairs and I introduced Barbara.

David had brought along a medium-sized football he found in his kitchen closet probably left there by one of Darla's sons the year David had let that family stay at his house.

David tossed it Hassan saying, "It's actually football season now--maybe you and your dad can pass..."

Bill said, "No-- I don't know anything about football-- you pass with Hassan."

When David tossed the ball to Hassan, the boy, not knowing how to catch, it bounced off his chest. Although pale and delicate-looking, and although eleven years old, he was the size of an average American eight-year-old. However, he was fearless, gentle and polite-- played soccer in the alleys of Kabul while bombs fell all around...Children can get used to anything if forced to, David thought-- a survival mechanism.

David showed Hassan how to properly hold the ball to throw and catch it while Barbara chatted with Bill.

That week on CNN it was reported that the Taliban had kidnapped the eleven-year-old son of a prominent businessman and held the boy for ransom. When the father couldn't pay the exorbitant amount demanded by the kidnappers, the *horrorists* beheaded the boy and stuffed his body in a trash can.

David said to Bill, "I'm sure glad you got this little guy out of that horror," putting his arm around Hassan's shoulders.

David and Barbara cut over to River Front Park path and walked along for several blocks, the river sparkling like diamonds.

On the way back they ran into Hassan and some African-American boys tossing footballs around. Hassan, smiling, tossed his ball to David who tossed it back saying, "I'll see you again."

Barbara commented, "What an *enchanting* child!"

While at WalMart the following week David decided to buy a size eight San Francisco 49ers jersey for Hassan who had liked the red and gold colors on David's jersey he had worn on his and Barbara's visit.

The following Sunday was another glorious sunny October temperature in the 70s.

Hassan was delighted with the jersey which fit him perfectly. The parents were appreciative of David's generousity as they had left Kabul with just the clothes on their backs and the kids had to leave their toys behind except for Hassan's soccer ball.

After chatting with Bill for awhile, David passed the football around with Hassan and showed him how to kick and punt it. The boy was enthusiastic and a quick learner.

The next weekend, the first in November, David took the train to Oakland where Barbara picked him up at the station and he would spend the weekend. That Saturday evening, after a challenging five-mile hike in the mountains, Barbara prepared a delicious meal of grilled salmon, parsley potatoes, steamed broccoli, garden salad with light Italian dressing and a scrumptious peanut butter cheesecake. David downed most of the bottle of Paul Masson Rose, fortifying himself (feared rejection again) enough to tell Barbara about his *cardiac arrest* in September.

When David was finished and somewhat weepy, Barbara asked, "You mean they're going to send you to prison for buying someone a baseball cap?"

"Well--no, they can't do that so they *had* to find *something* to charge me with-- so they charged me with not listing my pen name, that they call my *alias.* when I registered for Megan's Law."

"That's ridiculous!," Barbara said and took a large swig of wine.

Barbara had been hinting that their friendship should become intimate-- sexual.

David hesitated as he wasn't attracted to her in that way and it would change the relationship irrevocably if he complied. He should have discussed it with her though, as he kept putting her advances off which she took as a personal rejection of her female attractiveness.

It began to cause a strain on their relationship that brought out repressed resentments against David (she never married and had several failed relationships after the death of Dr. Patchin-- seemingly attracted to

Gay men) that expressed itself in the occasional biting, snide remarks that hurt David. She confessed that she was already having an affair with a married man who *visited* once a week. So David wondered why she kept up the sexual innuendoes unless it was because she found him more attractive or a challenge, as some women do when faced with a man that doesn't immediately respond to their advances. But for David the chemistry was just not there even if he had tried Viagra that he soon found out was illegal for convicted sex offenders to purchase in this state anyway.

The previous Sunday David had visited the Afghan family and passed and kicked the football around with Hassan who when he saw David approaching yelled excitedly, "Dave is here!" Hassan asked whether David had one of those things you set the football on to kick it. David said he'd check and if not he'd bring one (a tee) on Veteran's Day knowing Hassan would be off school.

Veteran's Day was cloudy, windy and chilly but David had promised Hassan he'd bring a tee. No one was outside so David went up the stairs to their second floor apartment and knocked on the door. David noticed the row of shoes from largest to smallest sitting outside the door, a custom of Moslems that you remove your shoes when entering a house. The door opened and Hassan and Bill came out wearing their coats.

David explained that he had promised to bring Hassan a kicking tee and brought it out of his pocket and gave it to the boy.

Bill said that "Hassan has been sick the last few days and we're going to the North Santa Losa Children's Clinic (that was an extension of the North Santa Losa Medical Center that was conveniently only a block away) for tests."

David, concerned about Hassan whom he'd grown quite fond of asked if he could come along.

"Of course," Bill said.

The clinic part of the medical center was for low income and welfare recipients. Bill could not find a job because of the economy-- it being even harder for him as an immigrant and it was also demeaning for him in his Islamic culture to not be able to support his family and what he looked upon as handouts. On the way to the clinic Bill said he didn't know what he was going to do if Hassan had something serious that required an operation or long-term treatment. David offered to help Bill if the need arose.

Bill said, "I'm sorry, I couldn't accept that."

After waiting almost an hour in a small waiting room with crying babies and coughing toddlers, Hassan and Bill were called in to see the doctor where blood and urine samples were taken from Hassan.

On the way back to the house David told Hassan he hoped he'd feel better and if he was OK next Sunday he'd come and he's show him how to use the kicking tee.

Sunday arrived and it was a very nice sunny late autumn day. David stopped in to see how Hassan was doing. Hassan must have saw him coming as he bounded out of the house and ran up to David. David showed Hassan how to position the football on the tee at the proper leaning angle laces facing out. Hassan soon mastered the technique and had David chasing the football after it sailed over his head.

Bill came out and said it was time for Hassan's shower and said the results of the tests showed it was just a stomach virus to Bill's (and David's) great relief.

A few days later David had taken his usual afternoon walk home from city center and stopped at the Santa Losa Pharmacy to pick up his prescription of Lovastatin he took for moderately high cholesterol. The pharmacy happened to be on part of the first floor of the North Santa Losa Children's Clinic where Hassan had gone for tests and was only a block from his apartment in the Riverview Apartments.

When David came out the door of the pharmacy after picking up his prescription he heard and saw a commotion on the corner. What he saw shocked and angered him. Three African-American boys (American-size 11-year-olds) were chasing Hassan and Minaya screaming, "Terrorists! Go back to Afghanistan!"

David was about to intervene when the three boys stopped and turned south on 33rd Street and Hassan and Minaya ran safely home.

The weather in late November turned colder and blustery so there would be no more passing football due to the state of Hassan's delicate health.

David stopped in to see the family the following Sunday and Bill told him that because of the bad schools and harassment suffered especially by

Hassan and the lack of jobs, they had accepted an offer from an Islamic sponsor near Detroit to move there. Evidently there was a large immigrant community of Afghans living there and a job for Bill was promised. Bill said they would be moving after the first of the year.

David said he would miss them and that he had learned a lot from Bill about the truth of what was going on in his country-- that there would always be chaos in Afghanistan as there was no benevolent dictator that could unite all the factions: Sunnis, Shiites, secularists, atheists, tribes and the Taliban. Ironically, the only unifying force in their turbulent history was when there was agression from other countries as the British in the 19th century, Soviets in the 1980s and currently the Americans supposedly hunting for Osama Bin Laden while trying to democratize the country that will never happen.

David received a post card card from Hassan in January 2010 read:

> "Dear Dave, thank you for teaching me American football. I show my friends here. I like it here. People friendly. Your Friend, Hassan."

26.

David visited Barbara in late November and into December. She came to Santa Losa on a Saturday in mid-December to attend the excellent theatre group NewHouse's production of the controversial play *Doubt* about a priest in a Boston primary 1950s school who had been accused by an elderly conservative nun of seducing a student who, happened to be African-American and Gay, physically abused by his macho father and bullied by students at two previous schools and forced to leave. The mother of the boy was not concerned about her son being in a sexual relationship with the priest as much as pleased he had found an adult who could understand and relate to him. Unfortunately the suspicious nun forced the priest to resign and the mother took the boy out of the school when she found out what the nun had done. There had been no proof of any intimacy between the priest and the boy. At the end of the play the old nun racked with guilt and regret confesses to a younger nun, crying, "I have doubts!"

The following weekend David visited Barbara and having drunk a little too much Paul Masson Rose, told her about his friends the Afghan family moving in January and rather tearfully said how much he's missed Hassan and loved him as a grandfather would. Just like Tommy both boys had lost their own grandfathers in recent years and David fell into that role if only briefly, in their lives.

It did not occur to David at the time that Barbara was actually *jealous* of his *love* for Hassan and this fact would later have a dire effect on David's prison sentence.

Barbara visited David one more time between Christmas and New Year's and they attended another play of the NewHouse thespians, *A Christmas Carol.* After the play they went back to David's house. They were sitting on David's couch talking when Barbara noticed the 8 x 10 photo of Hassan that David had enlarged and framed and that was taken on that last Indian summer day in November that they had passed and kicked the football.

Barbara frowned and asked rather sarcastically, "YOU have a photo of Hassan prominently displayed on your table without any other photos?"

David just smiled and said nothing.

Barbara said, "It's time for me to leave."

David hugged her goodby and she said, "That felt like a *stick*."

"David just replied, "Sorry, I guess I'm bony."

In early January David called Barbara and offered to visit and Barbara said she was pretty busy that Saturday but he could come and she'd pick him up at the Oakland Public Library at noon. David often visited this library to do research for a new book he was working on.

David waited outside and was about to think she wasn't going to show up as she was twenty-minutes late. The he saw her walking toward him from a block away. Once in the car Barbara was silent except to say that she could only have lunch with him as she had a lot to do at her house (David thought that probably her once-a-month *slam bam, thank you ma'am* lover was due that afternoon). David could tell something was wrong as he could feel the chill between them and asked but all he got was stone silence. She finally "Are you really going to have to go to prison?"

David said, "Yes, probably next fall, but what's wrong, you already knew that was inevitable."

David asked again and again but Barbara only answered, "IF I say I'll just start to cry."

David tried again during lunch to find out what was wrong but got nowhere and he was becoming irritated. She deflected his questions by asking about how Hassan was. David said they had moved as he had already told her they would. She said no more an dropped David off at the train station.

David was only to find out much later that Barbara had signed the guest register at St. Mark's when she had attended services with David back in July. Unbeknownst to David the NNSP (neo-Nazi sexual police, e.g., the Santa Losa Police) had finally decided to further investigate David for their Discovery Package (evidence for his attorney to see) and had contacted Barbara. Evidently in a state of part jealousy and part fear of the police she had told them about his *love* for Hassan and *that's* why she acted so weird on David's last visit. Whether the police had ever contacted the Afghan family he didn't know but the police would use that purely platonic grandfatherly relationship with Hassan for a behind-the-scenes justification to seek a harsher sentence at which they succeeded.

David never contacted Barbara again.

27.

Improbable cause and lack of intent.

For four months the prosecution had not presented David's attorney with the discovery package. For those not familiar with the legal process in Amerika (where one in ten people are incarcerated feeding $ into the Prison Industrial Complex) the so-called discovery package is what "evidence" the DA's office claim they have produced.

During his court appearance in January 2010 David's attorney asked for a continuance as he had just received the discovery package this morning and hadn't had time to review it so the judge granted the continuance.

Unbelievably, the DA wanted a 10-20 year sentence.

The Affidavit of Probable Cause was the central component of the persecution's (sic) case and was spun and cleverly worded with omissions and stereotypical and profiled implications.

> *Your affiant is Trooper Max W. Trilling. I have been employed with the State Police for eight years. I am currently assigned as a criminal investigator, Troop N, Santa Losa.*
>
> *Detective Ralph Hellner, Santa Losa Police Department, reported that he was advised of suspicious activity by the Defendant who identified himself as Daniel ESPOIR. Upon investigation Detective Hellner reported the following: after socializing with a young boy and his mother at a Santa Losa Indians baseball game in June 2009, the defendant arrived at St. Mark's Church in Santa Losa from mid-July to the beginning of August 2009.*

> *The defendant was attempting to locate the young boy from the game, who attends the church. Upon his arrival to the church, the Defendant identified himself as Daniel ESPOIR and signed a guest card with the name Daniel ESPOIR. The Defendant also provided personal business cards presenting himself as a freelance writer by the name of Daniel ESPOIR. One business card had information concerning a journal written by Daniel ESPOIR; The Better Angels of Our Nature. A search of the internet produced information concerning several books being advertised for sale by the author, Daniel ESPOIR. The books were published between 2005 and August 2009. Megan's Law Registration records verified that the Defendant last verified his personal information on 5/20/2009 at the State Police Barracks, Santa Losa. The Defendant failed to provide information concerning his alias that date.*

David noted several distortions and falsehoods in the *Affidavit*: (1) "suspicious activity by the defendant." *What* is suspicious about wanting to repay the mother and boy's kindness at the game with a copy of the excellent photo? (2) "Attempting to locate the young boy." David was not attempting to locate the young boy just the mother to give HER the photo and thank her for her kindness. (3) "Young boy who attends the church." The mother and do NOT attend the church, just the school next door that wouldn't open till September 2009. (4) "Defendant signed guest card, identified himself as Daniel ESPOIR, and business cards..." David had been using his pen name since the early 1970s, NEVER used in for criminal purposes, and his book *The Better Angels of Our Nature* was being released August 3, 2009 and he was simply promoting it much as Samuel Clemens did as Mark Twain when one of his books was being published. Furthermore, David never thought of his pen name as an "alias" and wasn't trying to deceive anyone. If David had thought of his pen name as an "alias", he would have gladly listed it at registration. It was simply an OVERSIGHT, NOT INTENTIONAL, NO CRIME, NO PROBABLE CAUSE FOR ARREST.

The following Monday David went to his attorney's office. Donkle had reviewed the Affidavit of Probable cause and said the 10-20 sentence the persecution wanted was totally unacceptable and said they will ask for a trial by judge at the court appearance in March.

David read his own copy of the Affidavit of Probable Cause and mailed Donkle a copy of the distortions and falsehoods he found in it.

David met briefly with Donkle before the next court appearance in March. That meeting was when Donkle made a disrespectful accusation and untrue statement (in front of an elderly woman secretary of his), "You're doing the same fucking, perverted stuff you did before." He was obviously referring to David's relationship with Jamie in 1997 that the psycho-legal profilers labeled "grooming".

David angrily retorted, "How can you say that? All I did was try to repay the kindness the boy and mother had shown me (the pariah) at the game by buying the kid a baseball cap and later at St. Mark's wanting to give a copy of the excellent photo of the two I took at the game. There was no grooming, no inappropriate fantasies about a relationship!"

Donkle countered that David was in "denial" and that he had talked to David's long-time clinical psychologist friend Dr. Williams on the phone and contended he said that.

David confronted Dr. Williams and he denied saying any such thing to Donkle and had only talked to him a few minutes and believed David didn't groom or have inappropriate fantasies about Tommy and also didn't intentionally neglect to list his pen name as an alias at registration.

Donkle's demeanor and attitude with David seem to now mirror the *pedophobia*, stereotyping and profiling the persecution used based on false statistics of recidivism (actually 5.3% in three years according to a US Dept. of Justice and Dept. of Corrections study done in 2010). David felt, now too late, that he had obtained the wrong attorney. However, when he was arrested in September 2009, Donkle was the first one he thought of since he had "defended" David in the Jamie case in 1998.

At the March court appearance another continuance was granted till May.

At the May court appearance Donkle told the judge that David wanted a trial by judge instead of a jury trial. The judge told David he would be notified by mail or his attorney of the trial date. David told Donkle he felt he'd get a more fair trial by a judge rather than a jury that would be swayed by media-inflamed stereotypes of sex offender recidivism. Donkle agreed without comment.

Donkle called him a week later and said that due to summer vacations and a heavy docked load, the trial wouldn't be scheduled till fall.

28.

David had met an interesting gentleman at the North Branch of the Santa Losa Public Library. Tom had been a high school English teacher but said he retired early after a bit of *unpleasantness.* He didn't elaborate and David didn't pry, after all, David had certainly had his share of unpleasant skeletons in his own closet. They shared a love of good literature and David gave him a copy of *The Better Angels of Our Nature* that Tom praised effusively. Tom was in his early 70s but with youthful stamina and spirit.

They took long walks on the river path along the Wapinoma and discussed various authors they admired. James, with his New England accent was originally from Boston and a Red Sox fan but enjoyed baseball on any level and suggested they attend Santa Losa Indians baseball games on City Island in July and August 2010.

One of their most interesting walks was a guided tour of old Santa Losa Cemetery that included the graves of early politicians and mayors of Santa Losa, first settlers, pioneers and gold rush men from the East who settled there after their claims were exhausted.

During the spring and summer of 2010 David continued to have more instances of his inexplicable *kid magnet* encounters.

After the breakup with Barbara in January David took to taking frequent train rides (he always loved trains since he was a young boy when he would watch the old steam engines passing through town with their eerie, mournful whistles blowing late at night).

He frequently took the train to Sacramento where only a few blocks from the station he could walk to the Train Museum that had many examples of early and contemporary engines, mannikins dressed as conductors and engineers, displays with recorded histories of the various trains and railroads and various kinds railroad memorabilia.

Only a block away from that was the restored Old Town Sacramento with the Pony Express Office with an actual 19th century strongbox carried on the routes and the saloon owned by Doc Holliday.

He also attended baseball games of the Sacramento River Cats, a triple A (AAA) minor league team.

One afternoon as he was waiting in the station in Sacramento for the train back to Santa Losa he noticed an attractive young African-American woman and her small daughter The child was about three years old and the only child there. About fifteen other adults, male and female, white and hispanic, were also waiting. All of a sudden David felt something around his legs. To his surprise the little African-American girl was hugging him and looking up smiling.

David said for all to hear, "What did I do to deserve this?" Everyone laughed.

This was not unusual as David frequently experienced the phenomenon known as "kid magnet".

Oddly, instances of this seem to have increased since his liberation from his sabbatical in zoohell Shanksville in June 2008.

Several stood out.

Barbara and David were attending an evening game of the Santa Losa Indians on City Island and the stands along right field were sparsely filled that night. They were sitting on the very top row-- alone.

Out of the blue from the second row way down below came this small boy about seven straight up the aisle to where Barbara and David were sitting, plopped right down next to David and said, grinning, "We were passing ball in my back yard before we came to the game."

David, nonplussed, said, "Oh yeah-- that's nice."

David looked over at Barbara who smiled and said, "I see what you mean." David had previously told her about his "kid magnet" experiences which of course in the present suspicious climate of 2010 could be problematic.

A man, David assumed was the boy's father, called to the boy, "Come back down here and stop bothering those people."

The boy said, "Ok-- but I wasn't bothering them-- see you sir."

On another occasion when David was attending an evening game, a man with three kids; a girl about ten, boy about eight and boy about five, sat down next to David...the youngest next to David. The little fellow proceeded to scrunch close to David putting one hand on David's knee and arm around his shoulder all the while staring smiling into David's face. The father told the little guy, "No, leave the man alone, Timmy." Timmy stopped but continued to stare smiling at David. After a few minutes Timmy again scrunched close to David, again putting his hand on David's knee and said, "I like you." Finally, the boy's father, who introduced himself as Bob, made Timmy move and Bob took the boy's place next to David. Bob explained, "Timmy's very affectionate."

David replied, "This kind of thing happens to me all the time-- I guess I'm a *kid magnet*."

When the game was over David said it was nice meeting you to the family and said he was walking home.

Bob said, "We'll give you a lift home."

David replied, "Oh-- I don't want you to go out of your way."

Bob insisted saying it wasn't out of their way. The older boy whose name was Carl and his sister Cindy climbed in the back seat and Timmy was supposed to join them but instead plopped down on David's lap.

Another time, later in that summer of 2010, David had once again taken the train from Santa Losa to Sacramento and after one of his jaunts around Sacramento was waiting for the train back to Santa Losa. This time he was sitting on one of the benches on the platform outside the station when (although there were other unoccupied benches) this blond-haired boy about eleven or twelve sat down next to David and proceeded to tell David, "We're (evidently referring to the obese woman and girl who appeared to be in her late teens who were sitting nearby arguing and swearing) going to the Fireman's Parade in Redding-- my granddad is in it."

David said, "That should be fun."

The boy chattered on to David and David could not help but overhear bits and pieces of the argument between the boy's (his name was Chris) mother and older sister.

"Your father won't be out of jail for two weeks-- so there's nothing I can do about it-- I can only give you and Chris a dollar if you're hungry."

Chris looked at the two as if embarrassed by them.

"Chris, you and sis will have to split this dollar on the machine in the station," the mother said.

Chris and his sister when inside the station and each came back with a small Milky Way candy bar.

A few minutes later Chris's train to Redding was announced and as Chris got up to leave David gave him a $5 bill saying, "Get you and your sister something to eat at the parade."

Chris thanked David profusely and hesitated leaving, almost if he *didn't want* to leave David, then after his mother called him for the third time, ran and boarded the train. As the Coast Starliner pulled away heading north, Chris waved, smiling at David from the coach window.

David and his best friend Walt wanting to get away from the heat and noise of the city had on a few occasions that summer of 2010 drove to Condor State Park about 45 miles northwest of Santa Losa. The park featured a large lake for fishing and boating, hiking trails and a large spring-fed swimming pool.

On the last Sunday in August 2010 before the pool would close after Labor Day, David and Walt drove to the park to enjoy the cool water of the pool one last time. David had brought along a small foam-rubber football that was permitted to be passed back and forth in the pool. In addition to the exercise they gained from swimming and diving, the tossing of the football almost two-thirds the length of the pool brought additional exercise and it was just plain fun. David took a break from the fun, climbed out of the pool and sat down on a bench. A few minutes later a small dark-haired boy sat down next to him. Shivering with a towell wrapped around his small frame, the boy, who later told David he was eight, looked at David and said, "Cold!"

"Yes, you have to keep moving in the water." The water was piped in from a mountain spring.

David went back in the water and he and Walt began to toss the football, now water-logged, again. Immediately, David noticed the little dark-haired boy standing next to him in the water.

David said, guessing what the little fellow wanted, "I bet you'd like to play," and handed him the football. At first Christopher (as he told David was his name) couldn't get it to Walt but gradually with his determination and *heart*, he was able to throw as far as David. When David and Walt finally tired, David patted Christopher on the head and said, "Have a good year in school."

On the same day, in between swimming, diving and passing the football, David was walking the length of the pool and as he reached the shallow end he did a double-take. A blond-haired boy about ten, was coming toward him with a big grin looking at David as if he knew him. He was very pretty and had a strong resemblance to Jamie from 1997. As the boy passed him he said, "Hi!" and David replied with the same. David was visibly shaken as the boy had unknowingly reawakened emotions and desire long reconciled. David soon regained his composure and just looked at the incident as one more mysterious kid magnet experience.

There had been many other examples of the kid magnet phenomenon that actually started when he was 14.

He thought of one last outstanding example. In June 1980 David was early for the opening of the North Santa Losa Swim Club Pool and was waiting outside in the parking lot with 20 people or so mostly women with toddlers or young children, older children and teenagers and a few adult men. David noticed a young boy on a bicycle pull up. The next thing David knew the boy was standing in front of him and asked, "Mister, can you take me in. I'm only nine and you have to be ten to go in by yourself?"

David, not surprised, replied, "OK, but you'll have to put your towell by mine."

Of *all* the people waiting to go in the pool he had chosen to ask David. *Why*?

29.

David knew that in September he faced trial by judge and and another zoohell-incarceration-sabbatical. After all, he *was* guilty even if not listing his pen name on the Sex Offender Registry was an unintentional oversight. He hoped for a 2½-5 yr. sentence but there was no guarantee because of the profiling stereotyping political reality based on false statistics of recidivism.

He had taken two trips in the summers of 2008 and '09 and loved train travel so he planned to take the train trip of a lifetime. He made reservations on the California Zephyr that ran from San Francisco to Chicago, although he would board at Sacramento which was closer to Santa Losa. At Chicago he would take the Capital Limited as far as Pittsburgh then the Pennsylvanian to Harrisburg, the capital of Pennsylvania, spend a few days there then take a bus to Gettysburg where he'd visit the Gettysburg Battlefield. Then take a local train to Philadelphia, then on to Washington D.C. where he re-visit Lincoln sites. Then catch the Capital Limited again to Pittsburgh and Chicago where he'd board the Empire Builder that ran north to Minneapolis-St. Paul and west across the northern tier of the country the whole way to Spokane, Washington where it split into two trains one proceeding to Seattle, the other to Portland, Oregon which is the one he would go on. Then from Portland he would board the Coast Starliner to Sacramento then take a local to Merced and bus to Yosemite National Park where he had made reservations for a three-day stay in a camp ground cabin and would explore and hike as a culmination of his pilgrimage journey. The following is his journal of the trip.

Up before dawn June 2010 morning shave shower breakfast coffee tomato juice oat bran 12-grain toast with peanut butter...friend Walt picked me up & took me to Santa Losa train station to catch 7:15 a.m. Businessman's Special train to Sacramento...arrived in plenty of time to board California Zephyr named for Greek god Zephyrus "God of the West Wind"...train soon speeding east leaving florid California lowlands climbing into Sierra Nevada Mountains...sat in booth with fascinating elderly British woman who was a world RR traveler & told me colorful tales of her adventures on RRs around the world...asked me to get her a glass of ice water which I gladly did...her name was Marjorie from Bristol UK...then met Narsaya an attractive woman in her 30s from Sri Lanka who had just received her Master's Degree in Environmental Science from the University of Florida & was touring US by rail taking photos along the way to show family when she returned to Sri Lanka...very pretty & sweet person...met jolly Hispanic physician with large active brood including three-yr-old boy who was quite a character keeping us passengers in stitches with his antics...met Jewish family from San Francisco who were taking their two kids to a youth camp in mountains...very friendly & precociously literate children boy & girl about 10 & 11 respectively who were quietly absorbed in reading adult sci-fi novels...girl paused to tell me of her love of books when she heard me telling dad I was a retired librarian & writer...said she planned to be a physician...now climbing higher into mountains passing through Colfax California & Colfax Station RR Yard with many antique engines...climbing higher noticed patches of snow dotting June mountainside...passed through several tunnels including 6.2 mile Moffat Tunnel then reached top of range with view of famous Donner Pass elevation 6,939 ft...highway visible down below on left of Donner Lake & east end the site of ill-fated Donner Party's camp...passed through Truckee California where nice Jewish family detrained & Truckee Station yard with an old Southern Pacific caboose #1268 displayed...then descended into Nevada paralleling Truckee River passing picturesque isolated wooden lodge then out of mountains through glitzy Reno Nevada then along Humboldt River into amazing white sands consisting of alkali deposits... known as the Great Desert stopping briefly in the middle of nowhere with temperature 100+ outside the only things growing sagebrush larkspur & wild onions...then up into Wasatch Mountains of Utah passing westbound

Zephyr on opposite of ridge at 7,000 perilous ft....then paralleling Green River Utah that morphed into Upper Colorado River Colorado into valley & Grand Junction Colorado Station that was impressive with its contemporary adobe style architecture into wilderness passing monolithic red sandstone mesas...passengers then gathered at end of Observation Car to hear very pretty 60s looking banjo-playing folksinger croon train & peace songs a la Guthrie Dylan & others...passengers joining in singing old favorites...me sitting at booth with very nice looking Mennonite family named Miller from Ohio returning from vacation in California...father, mother two teenage boys girl about thirteen & little boy about eight who sat across from me...I started to take photo of him but he reminded me "I'll have to confiscate your camera if you take my picture...we don't allow it"...I told him I was sorry & had forgotten Mennonites & Amish do not permit a photo or "graven image" of them...passed by exquisite Red Rocks Colorado...met Matt a retired teacher who lives in Bangkok Thailand with Thai wife & has taught English in Thailand & Viet Nam elementary schools & said he was going to visit older brothers in Chicago while his health still permits...he's in his 80s & recommended what he considered the best book on Buddhism he's ever read *The Buddha in the Jungle* (that I later purchased & enjoyed very much)...met Carl a botanist & clean water expert who works at Yosemite National Park...heard of my friend Bob who was a trail guide for 25 yrs....small world!...Carl is also a recreational mountain climber who's off to scale Mt. Whitney paralleled Colorado River as RR cuts through Rocky Mtns. east of Colorado Springs...Colorado River rafters moon train as is custom on this section of river into Gore Canyon rapids then Granby Colorado Station & sprawling Denver at dusk...Glenwoods Springs Colorado crossed Missouri & Mississippi Rivers into stormy Nebraska night with heavy rain & constant flashes of lightning like fireworks lighting up sky to south train slowing to 15-20 mph. due to threat of derailing if tracks flooded from nearby Platte River that paralleled the tracks through Nebraska...announcement made that those having train connections at Chicago will have to wait a day...Amtrak will reimburse paying for passengers overnite stay & taxi to & from Union Station...I get $40 in cash for taxis & voucher for overnite hotel...very swank room with large bathroom bedroom & living & huge buffet-style breakfast with every kind of eggs cereals bacon ham sausage fruits juices & coffees when we get to Chicago...hotel is Embassy Suites...in the meantime train creeps through long Nebraska night-plains & arrive next morning in steamy humid Omaha Nebraska temperature in 90s as I step off train to stretch legs during layover...on to Iowa passing through Osceola with its huge 15 ft. carved wooden statue of Chief Osceola of the Seminole tribe...Osceola is an anglicized form of "Asiyahola assi" from a ceremonial Yaupon holly tea or black drink & Yaholi the name of a Creek tribe god intoned when the drink was served...met youngish erudite professor of English literature who taught Byron & was touring US from England...had lively discussion on Dickens whom I greatly admire...met very pretty friendly high school girl from a small town in Iowa who said she was on a Christian youth retreat & planned to attend University of Iowa to become an elementary school teacher she exuded wholesomeness sweetness & innocence...I felt very grandfatherly & protective of her...on into Illinois as rain & darkness closed in...then Chicago at midnite & taxi to Embassy Suites...slept soundly & had huge breakfast from aforementioned buffet consisting of scrambled eggs home fries Canadian bacon toast OJ coffee & fruit cup... had time to walk to Lake Michigan waterfront before catching Capitol Limited train to Pittsburgh...bought postcard of US Cellular Field where Chicago White Sox play then taxi to Union Station & hectic maze passageways to waiting area for Capitol Limited...met retired professor emeritus of history from University of Chicago who was my age named Diana born of immigrant Greek parents...very attracted to her!...slept most of time through rest of Illinois Indiana then nightfall into Ohio where I said goodby to very nice Mennonite family & gave the youngest son Charles a postcard of Lower Yosemite Falls with my name & home address on it & was very surprised to get a cute Christmas card from the little fellow & have exchanged Christmas card & notes with family ever since... they detrained in north central Ohio at about 3 a.m. where relatives would be there to pick them up...forget the name of Amtrak station as I was half-asleep...arrived in Pittsburgh at 5:30 a.m. & went to nearby Greyhound Bus Station for early breakfast & caught 7 a.m. Pennsylvanian train to Harrisburg...Arrived in Harrisburg...PA's state capitol about 6:p.m.... got cheap room in Alva Hotel across RR station parking lot...had greasy but good burger fries salad & ice tea at hotel first floor next to bar raucous crowd already drunk...next morning up bright & early sunny day walked the few blocks to river front told Susquehanna River wider than Mississippi at points...after inquiries caught #12 bus that stopped at foot of hill where at top was the National Civil War Museum...walked up rather steep hill at points...hill had scattered monuments to various wars and locals who served in them surrounded by groves of oaks and maples and open green spaces in between...arrive at top where I saw impressive museum edifice that reminded me of both the Lincoln Tomb and Abraham Presidential Library & Museum in Springfield, IL...paid $5 fee and spent hour enjoying various exhibits of artifacts memorabilia & illustrated depictions of battles & other events showing PA's participation in the Civil War walked down hill caught bus back to downtown had greasy meal of ham & green beans fruit salad & coffee...fell sound asleep in 2nd floor room occasionally awakened by drunks loudly arguing & banging doors...next morning grabbed breakfast of eggs-over-light home fries bacon toast OJ & black coffee energized for bus trip to Gettysburg Battlefield where hiking for miles over immense slaughterhouse...bus to Gettysburg ran twice a day leaving 8 a.m. back 4 p.m. took 'bout an hour...arrived at 9:10 left off at huge parking lot crowded with cars whose license plates were from all over U.S. Canada...entered new-looking Visitors Center with all the tourist trappings of gift shops food...walked 'bout half-mile through wooded path with crowds till came to vast monument-punctuated open fields of battle... wandered & wondered around haunted fields of death & glory till sense of ghost-sorrows too much...asked park ranger where site of Lincoln's Gettysburg Address said there's traditional one with monument & actual site at nearby cemetery...found it meditated there remembering Lincoln wore a strip of back crepe around his stove-pipe hat in honor of Willie's passing 16 months before at age 11...caught bus back to Harrisburg skipped dinner at Alva had already eaten at Gettysburg...sank into deep dream-filled sleep where I was fighting Rebels...had quick breakfast of egg sandwich black coffee just making train to Washington D.C. arriving at 10:46 a.m....left suitcase in station locker walked long Washington blocks to Lincoln Monument meditated there then stopped for lunch of turkey sub bottled water before trek to Oak Hill Cemetery in Georgetown & the Carroll Tomb where Willie lay from February 1862 till April 1965...a re-visitation hoping to re-experience that sense faint as it was of Willie's lost presence there & possibly another EVP...half-hour later I entered cemetery this time taking winding path to Carroll Tomb at far northwest corner instead of grave-whacking over old crowded graves drooping ancient vines ancient oaks...arrived at tomb...eerie silence except for bubbling brook at bottom of precipitous drop yet a peaceful spot...meditated caught vision of Abraham Lincoln his long frame stretched out length of narrow tiled-floor of tomb between wall of vaults & thick iron door Willie's coffin straddled next to him Abe gazing one last time at the boy's beloved countenance...as before put white rose in one of the square door slots & mini-tape recorder in another...would check when home if I caught any EVP...left that place of sadness & lost-timeness trekked downhill back through Washington late afternoon busy 2010 streets leaving 1865 behind in a memory-shrouded mist of fading mystery voices...waited at crowded mayhem station confusion for Capital Limited to Pittsburgh & long anticipated adventure-filled interesting people-filled journey return home to Santa Losa as journey East had been. grabbed a cup of java & bottle of H2O for trip...saw line forming for boarding Capital Limited... announcement made that seniors & adults with small children may go in front of line...David worked his way past some disgruntled passengers & helped carry bags of ancient but spry African-American lady he had been talking with...after long walk to their assigned car having to trudge up narrow steps to 2nd tier for seniors & adults with children they plopped down...the very congenial African-American lady was seated in the window seat next to David & said she was returning to Chicago after visiting relatives in Greenville South Carolina...across aisle sat a woman who was a dead ringer for actress Ali MacGraw when she played 1970 film *Love Story* & her son who caught me staring at his mom & smiled...I went to observation car as train headed northwest through Virginia then West Virginia forested wilderness arriving at Harper's Ferry where train slowed where "Ali's" son who told me his name was Jimmy & his mother's name was Janet joined me & Civil War buff gentleman at window where I explained to Jimmy about John Brown & his fight against slavery & pointed out the Armory building where Brown & his followers made a last stand against the troops giving the little guy a history lesson...on to Martinsburg West Virginia as it began to rain & passed old roundhouse in station...two seats opened up next to me & Janet & Jimmy joined me & introduced herself and said Jimmy had just turned eight this past April...

Janet very friendly almost flirtatious saying she was divorced & was a University of Illinois administrator...I replied I was a retired librarian & writer & blurted out she looked like Ali MacGraw in the ca. 1970 film *Love Story* with Ryan O'neal which brought a radiant smile that made her even more attractive & she said she was going to rent the film as soon as she got home...then Jimmy interjected that he loved trains (like Willie) & knew all the names of the different types of cars railroad equipment etc. which he precociously demonstrated naming out window as we approached huge Cumberland Gap Railroad Yard in the encroaching twilight snapping picture after picture on digital camera with that beautiful child-wonder & glee then pointing his camera at me Janet telling him to ask my permission first because that would be an invasion of privacy...of course I said OK & then and he said, "I like him!" & Janet said, "I do too!" & Jimmy said let's get his phone number so we can call him when we get home & I replied how 'bout I give you my e-mail address which I did Janet writing it down on a slip of paper (but stupidly I forgot to get her's)...I then mentioned my Civil War related book *Better Angels of Our Nature* based on the friendship between my great-grandfather Sgt. Charles Powers & Willie Lincoln son of the president. Janet wrote it down & said she'd like an autographed copy...I asked permission to take a photo of her & Jimmy which she granted and then wanted one of me & Jimmy which she took...I said "I feel grandfatherly!" half-joking & half-serious & Janet said, "You are!" & said Jimmy had recently lost his grandfather...twilight darkened into deep magenta then purple shadows then black night with only distant twinkling lights visible out train window through shadowed forest trees & mountains of West Virginia Janet said they were going back to the car & get ready for dinner & invited me to join them for breakfast in dining car in morning... before leaving Jimmy looked at his mom innocently suggesting "why don't you move back with dad & ______ (stepmom)?" Janet replied, "I don't think that would work honey"...I walked back to our car with them & they went downstairs to dressing & bathrooms to wash-up...I waited till they return & went myself & later bought tuna salad sandwich & green tea at canteen while they went to dining car...I can't afford dining car prices except for occasional breakfast...later talked briefly to both & said goodnite...Jimmy stretched out over two seats & Janet slept on floor underneath seats...can't imagine she'll get much sleep with pounding vibration of steel wheels on steel track all nite long...converse briefly with very nice elderly African-American lady me mentioning Janet & Jimmy & that wherever I go I seem to be a "kid magnet" & they spontaneously take a liking to me without my doing or saying anything to encourage them & mentioned incident at Sacramento train station platform waiting for train to Santa Losa with about fifteen people Hispanic white all adults except for very attractive young African-American woman and daughter about three-yrs-old...I watching for train looking down tracks when I feel something around my legs & it is the little girl hugging me with beautiful upturned smiling face...I looked at crowd and said, "What did I do to deserve this?" & everyone smiled & laughed...very wise elderly African-American woman looked at me smiling and said, "They sense the goodness in you"...I dozed off to the rhythm of the Trak wheels & the mystery of life love co-incidings & synchronicities of the All-Connectedness...up early next morning & shaved in small rocking bathroom pleased I didn't cut myself...wait for Janet & Jimmy to wake...Jimmy wakes first smiles & waves at me then Janet groggily crawls out from under the seats with hardly any sleep & they go to wash-up & then we head for dining car for breakfast where Jimmy orders what I order...huge thick special Amtrak Texas French Toast sausage OJ & Janet orders scrambled eggs ham toast grapefruit juice & we all order coffee too...later we meet in Observation Car where still drowsy Janet pulls out bottle of Red Bull & says this should finally wake me up...now were in Illinois...we had stopped briefly in Pittsburgh around midnite to pick up passengers than sped through Ohio & Indiana in the night. I had woke-up briefly at about 3 a.m. & noticed we were in Cleveland as we passed Browns football stadium lit-up in the night then through Indiana passing through Fort Wayne South Bend-Notre Dame U. into Illinois early morning misty twilight...Jimmy pointing out names of kinds of railroad cars & yard equipment again excitedly with youthful exuberant enthusiasm snapping photo after photo as we came to the outskirts of the windy city then Union Station Chicago...I help Janet & Jimmy's voluminous luggage out of car into maze of mega-station rush rush human chaos while Jimmy clamors for a souvenir shop but Janet understandably exhausted & wants to get to car in parking garage across from station...I insist on helping them carry luggage to garage & then final sad parting where I say emotionally sincerely, "I wish you two were going to Yosemite with me"...

Janet clasps my hand squeezing it saying, "It was very nice to meet you" & Jimmy hugs me twice (KM co-inciding!)...wonderful mother & son & I wondered can one really fall in love at first sight? seems so!...I could have kicked myself later for not getting Janet's e-mail address as I never heard from her...probably lost the little piece of paper I had scribbled mine on... have two-hour wait for Empire Builder train so I go to McDonald's & have a grilled chicken sandwich with mayo lettuce tomato & green tea then find my way through three-level maze of station to bench opposite tracks where Empire Builder will leave from people watching all the hurrying scurrying to somewhere anywhere nowhere?...board Empire Builder heading north paralleling Lake Shore Drive & Lake Michigan passing by huge cemetery where famous early 20th century Irish novelist James T. Farrell noted for his "Studs Lonigan" books chronicling life in late 19th & early 20th century Irish ghetto is buried then continued north into Wisconsin Milwaukee in heavy night rain where young girl in 20s gets on & sits next to me jabbering & whining on cell phone about boyfriend trouble all the way for an hour till Madison where she gets off (thank God!) in rainy night cell phone still glued to her ear like some obscene cancerous growth from her lobe...drift off to sleep & wake somewhere in foggy green-green countryside...cross Wisconsin River at Wisconsin Dells Station but only seedy part of famous resort & park visible...a string of casinos...continued northwest to Wisconsin-Minnesota border divided by Mississippi River as rain finally stopped & a gorgeous sunset appears with every conceivable spectrum of shades of red-orange-purple over placid blue water...through black night northern Minnesota wild forests hiding Native American rezs (reservations) of Oglala Sioux & many others & reminded me of orphaned full-blooded friend Jim West who along with sister had been "kidnapped" by US Govt. officials at age 10 & 8 respectively from rez & placed with great culture shock in separate Anglo-white suburban families...woke up in North Dakota where train picked-up a few passengers at Devils Lake Station unique, Western & old looking...then endless-seeming North Dakota prairie with isolated forlorn still-standing 19th century pioneer sod house ruins with nothing else visible but prairie grass all reminding me of *Little House on the Prarie* TV series...passed through small town whose name I forget with 1950s "Bullet" train #3059 sitting in yard...paralleled Missouri River for a while passing Lewis & Clark monument in high bank on left...

hilly terrain unchanged since Lewis & Clark's journey through here 200 yrs. ago...crossed into Montana prairie with odd probably glacier rock formations...then same endless prairie as Dakota with same lonely sentinel-like sod house ruins punctuating the vast big sky emptiness interminable monotony scenery broken finally with lively conversation with new train friends...attractive ladies in their late 50s...Joan a teacher of gifted kids & Maria a retired University of Iowa college administrator & marathon bicycle rider who said she was taking train to Seattle where she's meeting friends for marathon ride back across Washington state Idaho Montana & North Dakota cutting south through Nebraska to home in Iowa...across Observation Car seat from us three lively boys with laptops (21st century toys!) played video games...two obese boys about 10 gobbling bags of chips & sodas with obese parents sitting in both in front nodding approvingly contrasted by other boy about same age in pajamas who came from sleeper car to join playmates was eating yogurt & drinking green tea...I impressed patting him on back remarking "eating healthy... good!" He smiled & said agreeing... "yes!"...Joan & Maria noticed too & remarked two obese boys & parents were headed for diabetes-strokeland if not already there...passed through several small towns with wild West names such as Wolf Point & Snake River but looking all the same along tracks with junked cars bars & cheap motels...Maria relates story of woman on same train last year who got off hoping to find a cowboy for a "quickie" in motel & lost track of time & came running as train was leaving but too late...Amtrak policy is no waiting keep to schedule so woman was stuck there till train came next day same time...prairie now beginning to give way to foothills of Rockies peeking through increasing cloud cover horizon...passed through Cut Bank Montana that has worst temperature extremes in lower 48 states with 109 degrees Fahrenheit in Summer & -47 degrees Fahrenheit in Winter... train on high bank trestles overlooking town of Cut Bank (about a dozen houses) below in gully-like small valley...in distance to the North about five miles I could see fairly good-sized town of Browning Montana the American headquarters of the Blackfoot Native American rez...a tribe never conquered who fled back & forth from U.S. & Canada in 19th century & who were & are fiercely independent warriors...now in actual foothills of Rocky Mountains crossed Flathead River named after tribe that shaped children's skulls from birth in a way that the tribe considered attractive & were bitter enemies in past of Blackfeet...now into scenic Glacier National Park towering snowcapped mountain vistas on either side of Observation Car...passed quaint Glacier National Park Lodge where one can stay & have guided tours or the adventuresome can hike the many marked trails of varying difficulty...deeper into the park mountainsides higher & increasingly steep as train cuts through valley...amazing how tracks were carved practically by hand by thousands of Chinese & Irish workers just like Union Pacific...many hundreds dying in process from dynamite accidents & rock slide avalanches...passed clear glistening azure mountain Lake McDonald...National Park Service tour guides entered Observation Car with huge plastic relief map of park & did a masterful job of telling history of park & pointing out geographical highlights...I snapped photo of group of elk perched on mountainside...dusk-shadowed peaks then darkness & I returned to my car as we crossed through Idaho "chimney" forest mountain wilderness-blackness...& into Washington state...that same evening two US Border Patrol officers came through train asking people if they were US citizens...asked me if I was & I said yes and offered ID but they said not necessary...later saw them take two guys away in handcuffs...all post 9/11 Homeland Security madness as we're only a few miles from Canadian border...fell asleep and woke up to morning sunshine Pasco Washington Station...grabbed coffee OJ & small box of Raisin Bran while passengers boarded & deboarded...train had split at Spokane Washington during night with half containing dining car continuing to Seattle & my half with canteen & new engine headed for Portland Oregon...entered picturesque Columbia River Gorge with tracks running along side right bank right above water...magnificent vistas of high wooded cliffs in mist & wide deep river empty of boats except for one passing Mississippi River-like steam tour boat...giant wind turbines reminding me of tripod monsters in 1950s sci-fi classic film *War of the Worlds* on bare tops of cliffs on Oregon side of river...sat with two new sixtyish lady travel companions headed to Seattle via Portland stopover... Janice a retired banker from Illinois tall reserved & dignified & Melba retired banker from Germany petite rotund & jovial both widows...finally arrived at bridge over Columbia River at Vancouver Washington after passing mansion-like upscale homes lining Washington riverside...crossed bridge into Oregon then a few miles later arrived at Portland Amtrak

Station…as it turned out Janice & Melba should have moved to Seattle cars at switch in Spokane as the next day they had to meet tour cruise liner headed up inland water passageway through islands by Vancouver British Columbia to Juneau Alaska but no problem as a connecting train to Seattle could be caught in a couple of hours so we decided to grab free trolley that ran to downtown Portland as I too didn't have to catch the Coast Starliner train to Sacramento for a few hours…we arrived downtown & walked to Willamette River that runs through the center of Portland & that I always mispronounced when it is pronounced WillAMette…passed Chinatown section with its big red & gold arch entryway & came to Willamette River Park & visited small maritime museum & headed back to center city & had lunch at Subway tuna salad sub & green tea & caught trolley back to Amtrak station…said goodby to Janice & Melba who gave me their e-mail addresses promising to tell me about their further trip adventures as I would mine…waited in line for Coast Starliner boarding till ushered to specific car that would go the whole way to Sacramento…attractive slim brunette with alluring green eyes sat next to me & we started friendly conversation…she said she was a librarian from the University of Oregon at Eugene and was on her way home to Eugene where she lived with her mother after a doctor's appointment to treat an ongoing medical condition that was quite painful at times…she's single looks 35 but tells me she's 50… name is Jeanette…told her about my library background & freelance writing since retirement…she impressed me as very nice person & since (2012-13) we have become pen pals)…before deboarding at Eugene she invited me back to Oregon & said she would show me the beautiful Oregon coast an hour or so away…God willing I'll make that trip someday… Oregon countryside green & lush then passed through nice-looking town of Albany then Salem Station with neat clock tower…Jeanette deboarded at picturesque Eugene Station we passed the University of Oregon Field where Prefontaine Classic Track Meet named after famed Olympic 1,500 meter track star from Eugene who died in a car accident tragically young before reaching his potential…annual world class track meet held there every year in his honor…I'd love to attend meet there as I had run the 880 yard & mile runs in high school & college and still was an avid track & field fan…I took some photos of winding Willamette River the train was paralleling then magnificent sunset over Cascade Mountains fellow passenger pointed out silhouetted spire of Mt. Shasta in gathering twilight in distance to west...gained altitude in southern Oregon forested darkness with occasional glimpses of terrain...cell phone says "searching for signal" as I try to call friend but forest too thick as we cross into northern California mountains now called Sisskiyou instead of Cascades then I fall into dreamland leaning against train-pillow on window & wake up in sunny Redding California then Modesto with its adobe-style train station on to Merced where I detrain & inquire where bus connection into Yosemite National Park is & am pointed to edge of station where smiling Black woman driver ushers us passengers on bus...comfortable bus is only half-filled & I engage young college student in conversation who says he attends UC-Berkeley & is traveling around during summer off from classes...a psych major & very nice young man...California flat farmland soon gives way to foothills of Sierra Nevada Mountains rising like mirages on horizon...winding up & up speeding around mountain curves driver assures us she's been doing this route for years very confident...arrive at beautiful quaint town of Mariposa (Spanish for butterfly) halfway up mountain...stop & stretch legs & think wouldn't mind retiring here friend Bob who was guide in Yosemite for years mentioned and I agree...Bob worked in beautiful Yosemite for over twenty-five years & hiked all over rough Yosemite north country with wife & son without incident only to have her die inexplicably & ironically in car accident in the Yukon while visiting parents in Whitehouse...Bob with sister as children had the exciting opportunity to be in the classic 1950s western *Shane* and meet & get autographed photos from stars Alan Ladd Jack Palance Virginia Mayo and play with Brandon de Wilde the young boy star who died tragically very young...briefly checked-out Mariposa History Museum then reboarded bus paralleling rough rapid-filled Merced River...excitement building as we approached park...pass Rainbowed Bridal Falls on other side of river on the right glimpsed through trees...begin to see stupendous views of towering granite rock formation known as El Capitan & Lower Yosemite Falls then bus slows to crawl as big line of vehicles of all sizes & descriptions creep into vast parking areas of park proper...perhaps vehicular traffic should be banned from park altogether as emissions are despoiling US national parks along with careless littering & tramping tourists...why not build a light rail system into park where road is now & return parking lots to the wild?...finally we de-bus & are told bus back to Merced will be here at 3:20 p.m....I take out map of park & orient myself with myriad paths rotating out in all directions...the many-languaged crowd sounds like imagined Tower of Babel...I head down path indicating it leads to Lower Yosemite Falls where I ask British couple to take photo of me with my digital camera perched on rocks at base of falls spray cooling me off in sunny 80s heat...breeze from falls blows off my Springfield Land of Lincoln cap that lands in falls' creek...I could have rescued it but hurry to gift shop instead & buy a Yosemite Half Dome cap (Half Dome being the 2nd most impressive solid granite rock formation in the park)...I take numerous photos of falls El Capitan which is the highest freestanding granite rock in the world at 3,000 ft. & smaller Half Dome...take photo of determined to survive miniature tree with exposed root system growing out of sheer cliff...fighting to survive like us puny humans everywhere & tree with cancerous-looking tumors growing nearby then stand directly under Half Dome feeling even punier...then stop at one of the several expensive snack bar convenience stores scattered around park for lunch of huge delicious veggie sub with bean sprouts spinach feta cheese black olives & tomatoes with green tea...sat with family from Michigan & had very friendly conversation... End Journal.

After lunch David headed up the Yosemite Falls Trail and found his cabin...got his backpack ready continued up the trail & camped the first night along Tioga Road opposite the east end of the Hoffman Range...he had brought along a copy of naturalist & explorer John Muir's *How Best To Spend One's Yosemite Time* paying particular interest to the section "The Upper Tuolumne Excursion" that will act as a trail guide & introduction to Tuolumne's unique flora...next morning he climbed Mt. Hoffman & then on past Tenaya Lake into Tuolumne Meadows & camped near Soda Springs...here in this upper Tuolumne Valley are the widest smoothest most serenely spacious views in all the High Sierras...it is the heart of the high Sierra east of Yosemite proper...eighty-five hundred to nine-thousand feet above sea level...the gray picturesque Cathedral Ridge bounds it on the south...a similar ridge or spur...the highest peak of which is Mt. Connors on the north...the noble mountains Dana Mammoth Lyell McClure & others on the axis of the range on the east...a heaving billowing crowd of glacier-polished rocks & Mt. Hoffman on the west...down through the open sunny meadow levels of the valley flows the Tuolumne River fresh & cool from its many glacier fountains...the highest of which are the glaciers that lie on the north side of Mt. Lyell & Mt. McClure... along the river he passed a series of beautiful glacier meadows that extend with little interruption from the lower end of the valley to its head...a distance of about twelve miles from which the glorious mountain may be enjoyed as the look down in divine serenity over the dark forests that clothe their bases...David passed through narrow strips of pine woods that crossed the meadow carpet from side to side...somewhat roughened here & there by moraine boulders & deadfall brought down from the heights by snow avalanches...but for miles it is smooth & level & he had no difficulty traversing it...The main lower portion of the meadows is about four miles long & from a quarter to half a mile wide...but the width of the valley is on average about eight miles...tracing the river David found that it forked a mile above Soda Springs...the main fork turning southward to Mt. Lyell... the other eastward to Mt. Dana & Mt. Gibbs...along both forks strips of meadow extend almost to their heads...David took the south fork toward Mt. Lyell...he came upon one of the few remaining river-lakes & a nice meadow to camp for the night...the sod in most places is exceedingly fine & silky & free from weeds & bushes...white flowers abound especially gentians dwarf daisies *Fotentillas* & the pink bells of dwarf *Vaccinium*...on the banks of the river and its tributaries *Cassiope* and *Bryanthus* may be found where the sod curls over stream banks and around boulders...the principle grass of these meadows is a delicate *Calamagrostis* with very slender filiform leaves & when it is in flower the ground seems to be covered with a faint purple mist...the stems of the panicles being so fine that they are almost invisible & offer no appreciable resistance in walking through them along the edges of the meadows beneath the pines and throughout the greater part of the valley...tall ribboned-leaved grasses grow in abundance...chiefly *Bromus Triticum* & *Agrostis*...the groves around Soda Springs are favorite camping grounds on account of the cold pleasant-tasting water charged with carbonic acid & because of the views of the mountains across the meadows...Glacier Monument Cathedral Peak Cathedral Spires Unicorn Peak & a series of nameless companions rising in striking forms nearness above a dense forest growing on the left lateral moraine of the ancient Tuolumne glacier which broad deep & far-reaching exerted vast influence of the scenery of that part of the Sierra...as he settled down for the night he was surprised to see approaching in the twilight two backpacks...a young woman & her small son they asked if they could join his campsite for the night & he said of course as he could understand that as glorious as was the daytime scenery of this place...the Upper Tuolumne region was isolated & few hikers made their way this far...David introduced himself as a retired librarian & author from Santa Losa...Cindy as she introduced herself said she was a professor of botany at Sacramento State University and her son Jarrod was ten...both were slim & trim with Nordic looking angular features blonde hair & blue eyes...Cindy added that they had been camping & hiking in Yosemite since Jarrod was five & it was their first time up this far in the Tuolumne Valley & she appreciated the company...Cindy asked what David had written & he said his Civil War related historical novel *The Better Angels of Our Nature* had been published last year...Jarrod peppered David with questions as whether he'd seen any bears wolves or mountain lions...David said no but he was sure there were some in the rugged mountains of North Yosemite..."We saw a black bear last year near our campsite at Soda Springs...it stole some people's dinner from their tent...I got a picture of it," Jarrod said proudly..."Cool," David replied...the Yosemite night chill soon forced all three into their tents & sleeping bags...the next morning Cindy & Jarrod said they were taking the east fork of the river to climb Mt. Dana...a fairly easy ascent from the west side where the trail is so gentle & smooth that one may ride a mule to the very summit at 13,000 feet...David said goodby explaining he wished they were going with him...Jarrod hugged David & said maybe we'll see you again...David watched them disappear down the trail...he missed them already...David turned southward above the forks of the river & entered the narrow Lyell branch of the valley...narrow enough & deep enough to be called a canyon...it is about eight miles long & from two to three thousand feet deep...the flat meadow bottom is about two to three hundred yards wide with gently curved margins about fifty yards wide from which rise the simple massive walls of gray granite at an angle about thirty-three degrees...mostly timbered with a light growth of pine & streaked in many places with avalanche channels...when he reached the upper end of the valley in early afternoon the Sierra crown came in sight forming a finely-balanced picture framed by the massive canyon walls...in the foreground were purple meadow willow-thickets on the river banks...in the middle distance huge swelling knobs of granite that form the base of the general mass of the mountain with fringing lines of dark woods marking the lower curves...As evening shadows approached David found a good campground on the east side of the river about a mile above a fine cascade that comes down over the canyon wall...the next morning David took it easy climbing leisurely to the summit of Mt. Lyell experiencing only one place near the top where he had to be careful negotiating a narrow ledge...the views at the summit were absolutely glorious...well worth the eight hours work...to the north was Mammoth Mountain Mt. Gibbs Mt. Dana Mt. Warren Mt. Conness & others...to the southeast the indescribably wild & jagged range of Mt. Ritter & the Minarets...southwest stretches the dividing ridge between the north fork of the San Joaquin & Merced Rivers & to the northwest extends the Cathedral spur...these spurs like distinct ranges meet at your feet...therefore you look at them in the direction of their extension & their peaks seem to be massed & crowded against one another...while immense ampi-theaters canyons & subordinate ridges with their wealth of lakes glaciers & snowfields maze & cluster between them...at this time of year crossing the Lyell Glacier is extremely tedious because the snow has been weathered into curious & beautiful blades sharp & slender & set on edge in a leaning position...they lean toward the head of the glacier & extend across from side to side in regular order in a direction at right angles to the direction of greatest declivity...the distance between the crests being about two or three feet & the depth of the troughs between them about three feet...the Lyell Glacier is about a mile wide & less than half a mile long but presents nevertheless all the essential characteristics of large river-like glaciers moraines earth-bands blue veins crevasses etc...while the streams that issue from it are of course turbid with rock-mud showing in grinding action on its bed & is all the more interesting since it is the highest & most enduring remnant of the great Tuolumne Glacier whose traces are still fifty miles away & whose influence on the landscape was so profound...David returned to his campsite that late afternoon satiated with the majesty of Yosemite & the High Sierras...he made his way down to his cabin & down the Yosemite Falls trail where he caught the bus to Merced... train to Stockton...bus to Sacramento where Walt met him at the station & home to Santa Losa.

The camping/hiking trip away from Santa Losa, away from people, away from the upcoming trial by judge renewed his spirit and hope that justice and truth would win out over stereotyping, profiling & enhanced punitive sentences based on false statistics of recidivism.

30.

On September 17 David took the train to Sacramento to take another of his long meditative walks around the beautiful city. At about 4 p.m. as he was waiting for the 4:15 train back to Santa Losa his cell phone rang. It was Attorney Donkle.

"I know the young female D.A. who was assigned your case and she agreed to a plea agreement of 5-10 years."

"Five to Ten years! What happened to two and a half to five?" His hope for a reduced sentence dashed. "What if we do go to trial by judge?"

"You won't be acquitted and they will go for a ten-twenty."

"I don't understand! You know it was just an oversight as far as the registration goes and just generosity to the boy."

"It doesn't matter *what I believe*-- they look at your past and think you were *grooming* the kid-- so you'd better take the plea or they will slam you."

"Five to ten is the same as some *actual sex offenses*!"

"I know but I can't do anything about it."

"When do I report for sentencing?"

"Ten a.m. Monday morning-- be at my office at 9:30 to sign the plea agreement."

David was hardly aware of the train ride back to Santa Losa. Zombie-like, he took the bus home, plopped on his sofa and stared into space until falling asleep hours later. All because he failed unintentionally to list his pen name as an alias and perhaps more so because he *dared* to be spontaneously generous to a kid by buying him a baseball cap--for an hour or two he had felt lese lonely-- a member of the human race again instead of despised pariah. Although he couldn't prove it, David suspected that Barbara's *attitude* and silence when he questioned her as to what was the matter was due to something he now remembered-- when she had attended St. Mark's with him she had signed the guest register with her address and phone number. He suspected that Detective Hellner in his investigation for the Affidavit of Probable Cause had called her inquiring about David. Barbara, acting out her jealousy (on one of his visits David, after a few after-dinner glasses of wine had stated that he'd grown to love Hassan as a grandson he'd never have but she *only heard the word love*) and in her anger and resentment at David for not being sexually attracted to her acted out her *woman scorned* by telling Hellner about David's friendship with the Afghan boy Hassan and that David had said he *loved* the boy. David knew right away how Hellner would spin that.

So, David concluded, his harsh sentence was NOT for his oversight of not listing his pen name as an alias but for what the persecution *imagined* David wanted to do with Tommy and Hassan. This absurd thinking ignored two facts: (1) The 2010 study by the U.S. Dept. of Justice found that of all categories studied, sex offenders have the second lowest rate of recidivism with 5.3% of offenders arrested for a new sex crime within three years of arrest. (2) Just like heterosexuals, Gays and Lesbians, MAPS (minor-attracted persons) are NOT attracted to EVERY boy or girl they see anymore that heteros are attracted to every person of the opposite sex they see, or Gays to every man, or Lesbians to every woman. The over two years that David was at home from June 2008 to October 2010 he saw pretty pubertal 12-14 with blond hair but purposely avoided them. Tommy who was eight and Hassan who was eleven but was the size of an American eight-yr-old did NOT turn him on at all but stirred grandfatherly feelings of affection.

Roger N. Lancaster, Professor of Anthropology and Cultural Studies at George Mason University in his ground-breaking book *Sex Panic and the Punitive State* points out that the tethering of punishment to imagined risks and anticipated future victimizations, as opposed to actual deeds and proven harm sets the law on a slippery slope.

A permanent pariah class of (s)ex-offenders sentenced to a lifetime technological scarlet letter by the Megan's Law protects no one.

All this knee-jerk overreaction is turning the American public into monsters, going panicky over anything remotely suspicious of being sexual, demanding apologies, precautions and laws that are unnecessary, at best Kafka-with-mad-cow-disease-esque at worst.

The various efforts of purging sex offenders from the community all re-enact the logic of social death: subjection or personal domination, excommunication from the legitimate social or moral community and relegation to a perpetual state of dishonor.

"If the only thing we do for MAPS [minor-attracted persons] is send them to prison, nothing about that can either erase those attractions or enhance the capacity of such persons to successfully resist acting. Unless we begin to appreciate that people in many instances need to be helped, not punished and chastised, not only do we do such persons a disservice, I think we do a tremendous disservice to the community as well."

Dr. Fred S. Berlin, M.D., Ph.D.
Associate Professor of Psychiatry
and Behavioral Sciences,
The John Hopkins School of Medicine
Founder: The Johns Hopkins Sexual
Disorders Clinic
Director, National Institute for
the Study, Prevention and Treatment
of Sexual Trauma

31.

A CARDIAC SENTENCING.

David reported to his attorney at 9:30 a.m. September 20, 2010 to sign the plea agreement papers and then go with his attorney to the courthouse for the 10 a.m. sentencing.

With great trepidation and anxiety, feeling like (if they sense it) a lamb to the slaughter--*a dead man walking*, they walked the one block to the court house. At his age with a five to ten year sentence, the substandard medical care and the general practice of the Parole Board to deny parole to sex or *sex-related* offenders based on false statistics of recidivism, or the current practice of paroling them but denying home plans padding their stats-- *we're paroling sex offenders,* he feared dying in prison.

David feared becoming once again a lost cipher in the cold blind maze of the Prison Industrial Complex.

But he also knew the court would slam him with a 10-20 if he forced the issue by going to trial-- a catch-22 situation.

David complained (while signing the rest of his life away) that the sentence of five to ten was equal or more than some cases of some actual sex offenses.

"I know," Donkle repeated, "But there's nothing I can do about it."

Arriving at the court house they took the elevator to the 4th floor and entered court room #4.

David was relieved it was empty (no spectators or more correct spectacle watchers) probably because the pseudo-Christian St. Mark's establishment didn't want any embarrassing publicity (David's sentencing was not reported in the Santa Losa Observer, either).

Only the judge, David's attorney, the young female assistant D.A., court stenographer and security person graced the gloomy room of injustice on this gray September day.

David felt like he was in a bad dream-- trapped, unable to wake up see a way out of the fog of hopelessness that was closing in on him. He scarcely heard the three players in his end game go through the motions of his near-death sentencing. When asked to respond he spoke mechanically, unfeeling shock cold stone turned inward to that safe dark womb-like sanctuary of denial, "This *can't* be happening to me."

SENTENCING

Persecuting Attorney: The State versus David Platon, 7816.cu.2009. Mr. Platon is present represented by his attorney, Mr. Donkle. Your Honor, I believe Mr. Platon intends to plead no contest. I will hand up the guidelines and Mr. Platon's history. As the Court will see, there is a five year mandatory minimum in this case and the State has offered a plea agreement for five to ten years in a State correctional institution.

It is my understanding that Mr. Platon intends to plead no contest to the one count of the information for that time.

The Court: Mr. Donkle, anything you wish to add?

Mr. Donkle: Only thing I wanted to add was the Court will recall we were scheduled to have a non-jury trial in this matter this morning.

The Court: Correct.

Persecuting Attorney: Your Honor, the factual basis for that charge is that the Court can see from Mr. Platon's record, he does have a prior conviction for involuntary deviate sexual intercourse from 1998, which would make him a lifetime Megan's Law registrant.

While he was registering with Megan's Law as he was required to do, it came to the attention of the State Police in 2009 that he was using another name, the name of Daniel Espoir E-s-p-o-i-r and that he was writing books that he has published under that name and failed to list it as an alias.

There is a sort of convoluted set of facts to how this came to the notice of the State Police, which I can give the Court if you're interested.

The Court: That's okay. Unless you want some of that on the record. I will leave it up to you. Do you need more information on the record? That's fine.

Mr. Donkle: The name isn't really an alias in the sense we normally think of it. It is a nom de plume and he had recently published a book under that pen name and had business cards printed up and had identified himself as that person much as Samuel Clemens did as Mark Twain and that appears to violate the letter of the registration requirements but in the usual street sense--

The Court: Very Well.

Persecuting Attorney: Sir, based on these facts, how do you plead to the charge of failing to register the accurate information regarding your alias with the State Police, guilty or not guilty?

David: No contest.

Persecuting Attorney: Will the Court accept the plea?

The Court: Yes. Mr. Donkle, anything you would like to add?

Mr. Donkle: I don't think so Judge. The plea agreement as negotiated calls for the statute-driven mandatory minimum. It is what it is. David has been educated as to the technical requirement of things, he may have listed-- said when he gave this Daniel Espoir. He has otherwise been free from any criminal conduct since his release in 2008.

His concern-- I think I should state it; because of his age and hopes to survive the mandatory minimum sentence and get paroled-- but the history of the Board in these matters is he is likely not to be paroled at the expiration of his minimum and he is worried he is going to die in prison [for an un-intentional oversight and loving kindness] and it is what it is.

The plea agreement as we have negotiated, is as *good as it gets* [enhanced sentence from misdemeanor to felony 2007].

The Court: Mr. Platon, you have the opportunity to speak prior to sentencing if you wish. You are not required to but if there is anything you'd like to say, feel free.

David: I accept the fact that I should have listed my nom de plume, however, I never thought of it as an *alias* and never used it for criminal purposes and have been self-publishing books under that pen name since the 1970s. I accept responsibility but it was not intentional.

The Court: Any other charges?

Persecutor: No, just this one count.

The Court: What's the provision?

Mr. Donkle: There is the statute 3819(a)3 of the Crimes Code and an amended insert, The mandatory is provided for in Judicial Code 32 9134.3 Subsection.

The Court: What was the book he published?

Persecutor: The Better Angels of Our Nature published [self-published] by WriterHouse August 3, 2009. Your Honor, since you are questioning it; it might be helpful if I provided some of the background facts of how this came to the notice of the State Police.

The Court: Maybe you should.

Persecutor: Mr. Platon was at a Santa Losa Indians baseball game where he began socializing [it was mutual] with a young mother and her son. During the course of the conversation he noted the mother was wearing a St. Mark's School tee-shirt. She indicated she was President of the Board of Trustees and her son attended. It is my understanding that Mr. Platon bought the boy a baseball cap [David told the boy to pay it forward and do something nice for someone tomorrow] and took a photograph of the boy [actually both mother and son with the mother's permission at the end of the game] and that was fine at that point.

Father Clement at St. Mark's began to take notice of Mr. Platon coming to services subsequent to this [baseball game]. He was speaking to parishioners there and giving his business cards promoting his book in the name of Daniel Espoir. [The same as Samuel Clements did as Mark Twain when promoting his books].

At some point Father Clement became aware of Mr. Platon's interest in giving the child [actually the mother] a copy of the photograph taken at the game.

[For some knee-jerk sex-panic reason] Father Clement became suspicious of Mr. Platon's intentions and checked the Megan's Law website an found Mr. Platon and contacted the Santa Losa police.

At that point all the information was put together and given to the State Police. I don't believe that additional contact was ever made after the baseball event by the defendant and the child.

The Court: All right. Mr. Platon, *I am sorry.* Was there anything you wish to say? Now is the time.

David: I wish to clarify some points made by the Persecutor First of all, I had been looking for a church in the area and was told by the mother it had a diverse congregation and even after I discovered the mother and boy didn't attend the church, *but only the school,* I continued to attend because I enjoyed the service and felt initially welcomed. Second, the photo I took at the end of the came was with permission of the mother and of *both* mother and son. It came out particularly nice and I wanted to give it to the mother out of gratitude for their kindness to a lonely old man who felt like a pariah. On the fourth and last day I attended services I brought the photo along to give to the very nice older lady who was the greeter when I first attended services in July 2009. Third, I unconsciously signed the guest register with my pen name as I was promoting my book that was to be released August 3rd and passed out business cards promoting my book much as Samuel Clemens did identifying himself as Mark Twain when a book of his was being released. Fourth, I also signed a card requesting a home visit where I planned to tell the Father about my past but that particular Father was on vacation so I was put on a waiting list. Lastly, There was no *intent* at deception and no *interest* in any further contact with the boy or his mother.

The Court: Pursuant to the agreement, at the sole count of information, the defendant is sentenced to pay the costs, pay a fine of $1,000 and is sentenced to a period of incarceration in a state correctional institution for a term of not less than 60 months nor more than 120 months.

Then David was handcuffed and shackled and driven in a van with eight other convicted felons to Pine Forest State Correctional Institution in the far northeast corner of the state where the Cascade Range meets the Sierra Nevada Mtns. He had known he would not be going back to Shanksville because of a DOC policy of not sending inmates back to a facility from which they had "maxed-out" (completed sentence).

They had taken his liberty but not his freedom, for that is a state of mind.
They had taken his body, but not his soul, for that is a state of spirit.
They tried to take his heart, but could not for that is a state of Love.
They had put him in the zoohell, but the only real hell is being unable to Love;
But boy, could he still love!

David Platon
Pine Forest State Prison
January 28, 2011